I0763384

ON THE RECORD

ANNA M. BOARINI

Cover design by MGSDESIIGNS

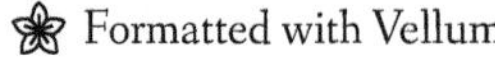
Formatted with Vellum

To the journalists out there pounding the pavement, speaking truth to power, and racing the clock to meet a deadline. Keep writing - we need you now more than ever.

"You're a newspaper man!"
-Walter Burns to Hildy Johnson
His Girl Friday

CONTENTS

Chapter

ONE

"Requesting backup. Two gunshot victims. EMS stat. I need backup!"

My police scanner crackled, and I shot up. *Two gunshot wounds? Here in Black River? What the hell is going on?*

I jumped out of bed and turned up the scanner, listening intently.

"All officers respond. Two gunshot wounds. 100 Route 11. Requesting all officers to respond."

100 Route 11 isn't too far from me. In fact, it's only ten minutes up the road. I grabbed the jeans I wore yesterday, as I shimmied out of my pajama pants. I nearly tripped trying to get into my pants as quickly as possible. I grabbed a sweatshirt off my desk chair and slipped it over my camisole —there was no time to waste on a bra. I ran towards my little kitchen, grabbing my backpack while I slipped my feet into my boots and grabbed my coat, slamming the door behind me. Thank God this is Vermont, where no one locks their door. I ran down the stairs and fished my car keys out of my coat pocket. I jumped in the car, rammed my key in the ignition, and was off.

The location of the shooting is one of the gems of southern Vermont. Bedford Farms, usually an idyllic dairy farm that makes cheese and famous strawberry rhubarb ice cream. And now it's the site of a violent crime. I jammed my foot on the gas; I wanted to get to the farm as soon as possible. Hell, I might even beat some of the cops.

Black River, population 5,000, is home to three police officers. There's the chief, Bernard "Bernie" Strauss, deputy chief Richard "Dickie" Weebaum III, and officer Jack Campbell. Jack is a new addition to the force, after the former officer got charged with drunk driving on the job and was subsequently fired. Bernie and Dickie founded the department twenty years ago. So, while it may seem like they've got experience, it's really only in the speeding ticket and lockout variety.

A shooting was something completely different. Nothing ever happens here, so something like this is big news. As the only reporter covering Black River and the surrounding areas, this was a big deal. I write for The Black River Recorder. I'm a staff writer, the lowest level of journalism, but I'll write my way up. And this story might just be a rung out of this place.

I hear the sound of sirens and saw one of the cops behind me. I pulled over to let them pass; I couldn't make out who was driving though. The minute they passed me, I revved the engine and took off. I needed to get there and figure out what was going on. There was a story here and I was going to cover it.

The car in front of me, sirens and lights going, took a sharp left down the entrance of Bedford Farm. If you take a left from the entrance, you head to the Bedford homestead, going straight gets you to the ice cream and apple cider donuts at the main shop, and a right takes you over towards the barns with the cows. I didn't know where to go, so I slowed down as I took the left and watched where the cop car went. They flew down the dirt driveway, kicking up some chunks of hard snow, heading towards the barns. I turned and flew down the driveway until I made it to the main barn and threw my car into park.

It was pandemonium. There were two bodies. One crumpled as if they fell straight down. They weren't moving and none of the officers were working on that person. Or I guess, the body that used to be a person. All three were crowded around another victim, who seemed to be alive. At least, alive enough to try and save.

I started snapping pictures with my phone immediately. Michael, my editor and owner of The Recorder, is usually the photographer, but we'd have to do with my pictures for this one. I didn't have time to call Michael and drag him out of bed for this. I was on my own. I got some pictures of the cops working. Dickie was near the head, while Bernie and Jack were on either side. I walked closer, hoping to get a better angle, when Dickie realized I was there.

"Alice! Get out of here! This is a crime scene!" he yelled at me.

I took a step back and switched to video; trying to take everything in. I ignored Dickie completely, pretending he wasn't even there. I kept filming. I needed all of this for the story.

"Alice, I swear to God, get the fuck outta here!"

This time the chief yelled at me. He scared me a bit, so I walked back towards my car.

"As a member of the press, I have a right to be here!" I yelled in their direction.

I'm not sure if that's legally true, but I was going to pretend that it was. I scrolled through my photos as I walked back towards my car and realized I had some good shots. I knew I needed to call Michael, but my attention was caught by the sirens coming in this direction. I watched as an ambulance screeched down the road, taking a precarious left to make it to Bedford Farms. They flew down the driveway towards the barn. As they parked, two people jumped out of the back with small duffle bags that I imagined held medical supplies. They rushed towards the person that the cops were working on, while a third person who drove pulled a stretcher out of the back.

I took some photos of the paramedics working. No one was paying attention to me, so I got pretty close. Close enough to discover the identity of the victim. Nathaniel Bedford was lying on the barn floor, surrounded by a puddle of blood. His shirt was covered in a deep red stain, while the puddle was growing underneath him. The paramedics were working quickly; they cut his shirt open to reveal the wound.

I stood there taking pictures, never stopping. But I knew I needed to call Michael. I walked away from the scene and hit his number. The phone rang and rang, but I didn't hang up. Finally, on what was probably the final ring before I'd get sent to voicemail, he picked up.

"Alice?" he said, his voice sleepy. "Why are you calling so early? It's barely six."

"There's been a shooting at Bedford Farm. It looks like Nathaniel is on the ground. I mean, there's blood everywhere. And there's someone else, but I'm pretty sure they're dead."

Everything came out in a rush. I realized I was shaking. It just hit me—this is the first time I've seen a dead body like this. Sure, I've been to funerals and seen someone in a casket, but never just laid out on the concrete floor of a barn, totally dead. My head started to swim and there was a roar in my ears. I felt like I was going to pass out, so I sat down and leaned back against the wheel of my car. I took a few deep breaths while dots speckled across my vision.

"What? A shooting? And someone's dead?"

Michael was definitely awake now. I heard the rustle of sheets and imagined he threw off his comforter and jumped out of bed, like I did only minutes earlier.

"Yes, I heard it on the scanner. Wait, something's happening. I gotta go."

I hung up and could hear Michael stammering on the other end, but I ignored him. The paramedics had Nathaniel on the stretcher and ran him towards the ambulance. In one swift motion, the stretcher slid into the back, they jumped in, barely getting the doors closed before they sped off.

We had a small clinic in town, but it couldn't handle a gunshot wound. He'd have to be airlifted up to DHMC in Hanover, the only nearby trauma center.

I took one more picture of the ambulance flying down the driveway before I turned back to the crime scene. Dickie and Bernie were talking into radios, while Jack stood over the body. I started to walk towards it when Dickie noticed me.

"Alice, I told you to get the fuck outta here. Do not come one step closer."

"What happened? Who's dead?"

Dickie ran a hand through his barely-there hair. He's one of those guys who's had a comb-over since high school. A million emotions flashed across his face. Fear. Anger. Disgust. Exhaustion. I knew he wanted nothing to do with me, but I was here, and he had to deal with it.

"Come on, Dickie. What happened?"

I whipped a notebook from my pocket and pulled the pen out of the spiral. I flipped to a clean page and looked at Dickie expectantly. He sighed. I knew at that moment that I'd won; he was about to spill.

"This didn't come from me, and you can't print names till we tell you. That's the only way I'll say."

I nodded. Here it was. My first major scoop.

"A little after 6 AM, officers responded to a shooting at Bedford Farms. Upon arrival, we found two victims. Nathaniel Bedford was barely alive, and we immediately started to work on life-saving measures. Byron Avery was dead when we arrived. As of right now, we don't have a motive or any suspects."

I wrote everything, my hand moving fast. I used my own version of shorthand; no one else would be able to decipher what I wrote, but that didn't matter. I was the only one that needed to be able to make sense of it. Dickie looked behind me and I turned; a car was coming down the drive. Michael's old Subaru. He threw the car into park and got out.

Michael wore what he always did this time of year—flannel shirt, jeans, and insulated rubber boots. He had a Carhartt vest on and a beanie tugged over his ears to fight the chill. I started to walk towards him, we met halfway between his car and the crime scene.

"What the fuck?" he whispered when I got close.

I sighed. That was the question of the hour. *What happened here? Who did it? And how was I going to find out?*

"All I know so far is Nathaniel is headed towards the clinic, Byron Avery is dead, and there's no motive or suspect. I can't release names, but everything else is on the record."

Michael shook his head, as if he couldn't believe what I just said. He's been reporting about Black River and the surrounding towns for decades. He was here during Hurricane Irene and still got the paper out, even though the newsroom flooded. He covered the Bernie Sanders presidential run, scores of other local political campaigns, and literally everything else there was to write about. He was the only reporter for a while, after his dad retired.

Mr. Cooper, Michael's dad, still wrote letters from the editor emeritus sometimes, but at eighty-five, he enjoyed retirement. Michael had been on his own for almost ten years when he hired me. Other than the football coach that covers the team, he'd been on his own doing everything for the paper, from reporting to formatting. He was a one-man newspaper machine. And then I fell into his lap.

I've been in Black River for almost three years at this point. I joined the paper right after college. Over sixty applications to papers all over the country went out, only two emailed me back—The Black River Recorder and The Bayou News. I got an interview with both and prayed one would take me. When Michael called and offered me the job, I jumped. I packed up my little Honda and moved a thousand miles away from home, for $15 an hour.

"Who'd you get on the record? Dickie?"

Michael's voice pulled me back to the present. I nodded. The chief started to walk over towards us. He reached out and shook Michael's hand and tipped his head at me.

"Bernie, what's going on?" Michael asked.

He was a worn-down man. He wasn't in uniform, rather in a get up similar to Michael's. Carhartt coat, boots, jeans, and a flannel. He looked over at me and his eyes were sad and tired. He looked like he'd seen too much. I knew better than that. The chief spent twenty years as a Marine; he'd seen some shit. But I'm guessing he never saw a kid he coached in little league, dead.

"This is off the record, but we haven't got a fuckin' clue. We got the call and thought the boys were messin' around."

I studied Bernie, my eyes slid from his face to the body lying on the barn floor. The cows had been bellowing the whole time we'd been there but were now silent. There were witnesses to the crime, around 100 in the barn, but unfortunately none of them spoke English.

"So, what now?" Michael asked.

"We wait for the state police. They take over from here, just like any other major crime. And they're gonna make you talk through them. I won't necessarily be able to get you the information you want."

He looked pointedly in my direction and my attention came back towards the two men. Both were old enough to be my father. It had taken time, but I'd earned their respect. It didn't happen overnight. The first time I interviewed the chief, he called me "whippersnapper." I didn't take too kindly to that and got him back. When the cops had to arrest a dog for burglary—*yes, that really happened*—I made sure it made front page news. After that, he realized I could play ball and I wouldn't pull any punches. Ever since, we've gotten along. He knows I want to report the news as best I can.

"Well, keep us as updated as you can. You know we appreciate it," Michael said and reached out to shake Bernie's hand again.

He turned away to walk back towards the crime scene when we heard the scream.

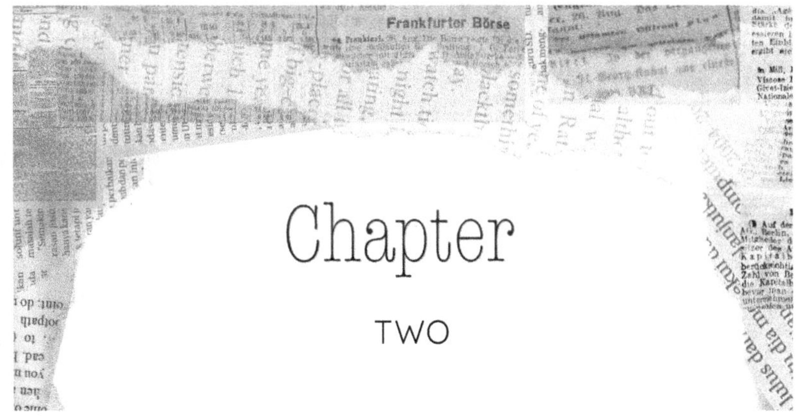

Chapter
TWO

Michael and I turned, looking for where the scream came from. Was something going on? Was the killer still around?

That's when I noticed Dickie walking towards the Bedford homestead. I followed. Something good was about to happen. And boy, was I right. Mrs. Bedford, Nathaniel's mom, Dairy Days pageant president, and former Miss Connecticut, ran towards the barn. Dickie was able to stop her before she got to the barn.

"Nathaniel! Nathaniel!" She screamed.

Mrs. Bedford is one of those women with everything in place. She wears pearls and sweater sets from L.L. Bean. This is Vermont, so she wears jeans and boots too, but I swear her jeans are pressed. Even in the depths of mud season, when everyone is filthy all the time, she's perfectly put together, nary a speck of mud on her person.

But this wasn't the Mrs. Bedford I was used to seeing. Her hair was sticking up in the back, like she had just woken up. There was a smudge of mascara under her left eye, and she was in pajamas. Matching pajamas with a monogrammed robe, but still pajamas. She lost a slipper at some point; her left foot was exposed to the remnants of snow on the ground.

"Mrs. Bedford, Mrs. Bedford, we've got him," Dickie said, trying to calm him down. "He's at the clinic and they're gonna get him to DHMC. I'll take you over."

She sobbed but nodded at Dickie. He led her over to one of the trucks. That's when I realized only the chief responded with his cop car. Dickie and Jack had their personal trucks. After getting Mrs. Bedford settled in the front seat, Dickie jogged over to the field that separated the barn from the homestead and picked something up. Mrs. Bedford's missing slipper. He knocked some snow off of it using his thigh and ran back to his truck. Moments after he got in the driver's seat, he backed up, swung the truck around, and was gone.

"Who responded first?" I said to no one in particular.

Michael looked over at me. I didn't notice it, but he'd got his camera out and was taking pictures. The click, click, click, of the shutter never stopped.

"Chief? Chief!" I yelled.

He turned around and started walking towards me. We met halfway.

"Who responded first?"

The chief gave me a wary look but still answered.

"Jack. He was closest. When we got that call that shots were fired, I sent him. It's Thanksgiving and I thought the boys were just shootin' skeet early, like last year."

I completely forgot it was Thanksgiving morning. The holiday wasn't my favorite, and I hadn't planned on celebrating, but everyone else in town would. Gail, the Black River Co-Op president, decorated the front of the store with pumpkins, gourds, and even a turkey made out of mums. I was supposed to cover the lighted tractor parade tomorrow. Everything was up in the air now though. Would we even have the parade?

"He called for backup?"

The chief gave me a look but nodded. He narrowed his eyes on me.

"What are you gettin' at, Alice?"

I didn't say anything yet. A timeline was forming in my mind, but there were still missing pieces. It was like I had the outline of the puzzle but was missing all the pieces for the actual picture.

"Who called 911? On the record."

The chief hesitated before he responded. I knew I only had a matter of time before the state police completely shut down my sources of information and I was going to use that time to my benefit.

"It was anonymous. We don't know who called in."

Bedford Farm was on the outskirts of town. The murderer—because that's what they were—must've gone north, out of the farm. We all came from the south, closer to town center. If they made the 911 call, they would've had enough time to call and leave or call on the way off the property.

"I think the shooter made the 911 call," I said almost to myself.

The chief immediately turned away from me and walked back towards Jack. I did the same, back towards Michael. I was about to open my mouth and tell him my theory when sirens split the quiet. We heard them before we saw them, but moments later, the green state police cars took the left and came down the driveway, heading towards the barn.

Michael got some shots of them arriving. When the state police parked, I recognized the Westminster barracks commander, who walked over towards the chief. Lieutenant Lyman Collins heads up the state police in our area, it made sense that he would be here on site. Other officers started to get out of cars and SUVs, pulling silver suitcases out of trunks. They started to set up a pop-up tent, where I guessed it would be mission control. Jack came over and helped one of the officers hang plastic sheeting on the barn door.

"What did the chief say?"

I filled him in about the anonymous 911 call and my theory about the shooter. He frowned. Just then, another van came down the driveway, this one marked Windham County Coroner. We were both silent as we watched the coroner walk towards the barn door. I was focused on the coroner and didn't see when someone walked up to us.

"Michael, Alice. I'll be taking care of all communication between the investigation and the press."

Well fuck.

Chapter THREE

Sarah Connolley, an information officer out of the Westminster barracks, stood in front of us. Like so many others, she was out of uniform. Her brown hair curled at her shoulders, and she wore leggings tucked into tall boots, with a long puffy coat. She didn't have a lick of make-up on but looked beautiful in the cold morning light. She was focused on Michael, but sent a glance my way and I felt my pulse quicken.

Sarah and I were—well I wasn't quite sure what we were. A few weeks ago, we went on a date. She was smart and funny, the worst quality about her is that she's a cop. She only joined the force because she wanted to stay close to home and help take care of her parents. She needed a good job and was able to put her Communications degree to work, while also making more than minimum wage and living close to home. She seemed great, like maybe I might make a friend or maybe something *more*. There's almost no one my age around here, let alone gay and not in a long-term relationship with kids. She seemed perfect.

We hooked up a few times and then last week, nada.

She ghosted me on a Saturday afternoon when we had plans. We were supposed to go to the movies, but she sent a text that she couldn't make it and then radio silence. Now I was going to have to deal with her. I don't know what I did, but I knew my job just got a lot harder.

"It's good to see you, Sarah. Wish it was under better circumstances," Michael said, shaking her hand. "Anything you can let us know now?"

She smiled and I felt like someone punched me in the gut. She was beautiful. And I was wearing yesterday's clothes and God knows what my hair looked like. I normally don't care what I look like, but now I was self-conscious.

Get a grip, I thought to myself. *You're here to do a job, not pine after some girl that wants nothing to do with you.*

"As of now, no. It's an ongoing investigation but keep your phones on you because we'll have a press conference at some point today."

She still hadn't acknowledged my presence and maybe that was for the best. Eventually, she'd have to talk to me. I was the reporter on this story. And she was my source of information. I kept looking in her direction, daring her to look at me. I cleared my throat.

"When do you think you'll have the press conference?" I asked.

She finally looked at me. Damn, those blue eyes were perfect. They were blue like the ocean in the winter, dark, unyielding, a depth I wanted to get lost in. I waited for her response.

"I'll let you know, Alice. We're not sure yet. As you can see, we just got on the scene."

Her answer was terse. Great, it was going to be like this. No information. Just tension. Michael looked between us, shooting me a look with a raised eyebrow, and I shrugged.

"I'm gonna give you two a minute and go talk with the Lieutenant," he said and walked off.

We stood for a moment, looking at each other. I scraped my boot against a piece of crusty snow. She flipped her hair over one shoulder and zipped her coat up against the chill.

"I need to know we can work together," I finally said.

She took a deep breath.

"I agree. We need to work together. I'll..." she trailed off.

We stood there awkwardly. This was my first major story and while I didn't expect her to give me everything I wanted for it, I still needed her to play ball. And I wanted to know what happened. I needed to be professional, but also, I was so confused. I thought we had a good thing. Even if it wasn't romantic, I thought I had made a friend. I cleared my throat again.

"Before we get professional and serious, I gotta know. Did I do something? If I did, can you just tell me?"

I sounded pathetic. I know I did. But I was curious. I mean, my whole job is to be curious about everything. And this was about me, so I wanted to know even more. She looked away and bit her thumbnail. Sarah was obviously nervous and uncomfortable.

"I mean, you don't have to tell me. I just wanna clear the air before this gets any weirder."

She nodded and finally looked at me. She seemed annoyed but softened her gaze.

"It's just...we can't be seen together. One of the guys saw us at dinner and reminded me that it's not a good idea to be involved with the press."

My heart dropped to my stomach. It wasn't that she didn't like me, it was that someone said something. What the fuck kind of elementary school shit was this?

"You ghosted because you couldn't be seen with me? I

know how to keep my personal and professional life separate. I'm not going to ask for quotes during pillow talk."

I could feel myself getting angry. I liked her. I like, liked her. Maybe it was desperation, but it was so great to talk to someone my own age, someone interesting and beautiful. I shook my head.

"Listen Alice, I'm the only woman in the barracks. I can't have them talking about me or thinking I'm not professional. I like you, but I can't risk my career."

I titled my head and just looked at her. I get it, I really do. No one took me seriously when I first started at the paper. I still get 'flatlander' thrown my way as an insult. I'm an outsider and I always will be. But I also don't give a shit. I can't change anyone's opinion of me. Vermonters are nothing if not opinionated, especially about someone that moves into town whose family hasn't lived there for eons. Black River was not some liberal bastion, either. We were a firmly rural, red area, and I had to contend with that daily.

"So, you're going to let the opinion of a bunch of meatheads determine your life? Really?"

She blushed all the way up to her hairline. I didn't want to hurt her feelings, but I also wasn't one to mince words. She was letting someone else dictate her life and I mean, I could sympathize, but *what the fuck?* She opened her mouth to speak, but I spoke first.

"I get it, it's not easy to be gay, working in a profession where a bunch of fucks don't take you seriously. I like you and I was hoping we could at least see where this would go. If it didn't go anywhere, maybe we could be friends. I've got no one here and I thought I finally made a connection. Obviously, I was wrong."

I went to walk away from her, but she reached out and grabbed my hand.

"Alice, wait," she said, pleading in her voice. "I like you too. I really, really do. And I wish it wasn't this way, but right now, it can't seem like you get special treatment because we have something outside of a professional relationship. Especially now. Can't you understand that?"

I fought the urge to roll my eyes. She was obviously upset about this. I wanted to understand. I mean, I went on a date with a cop. I gave her a chance, listened to why she joined the force, and didn't hold it against her. But here she was, holding journalism against me. It was hurtful. I liked her—not just because the sex was mind blowing—I liked her because I haven't laughed that hard in ages, because I finally felt something. I hadn't felt that way in years and I wanted to hang on. But I guess it wasn't meant to happen. I was still lonely and working all the time. Maybe this was my destiny.

"I get it. I can respect that. I don't like it, but I understand it. I hope that we're okay and this isn't going to be weird just because we've seen each other naked," I said with a smile.

She blushed again but shared my smile.

"We're good. I'm not going to be easy on you and give you everything you want, but we're okay."

I held out my hand to shake and she took it. As soon as she touched me, I felt a thrill in my stomach. I had it bad and needed to get over it. There was work to be done. A story to write and a murder to solve. Even though it was the cop's job to figure it out, my mind was already whirring with theories. I needed to know what was up in order to write the best story of my life. I had to beat the state police to the answers, because they sure as hell wouldn't give them to me.

"I look forward to working with you," I said.

We both turned back to the crime scene in time to see the coroner rolling out a stretcher with a black body bag strapped to it. Michael snapped photos and I walked towards him. We watched the stretcher get loaded in the back and the van drove away.

"Everything all right there?" He asked, bringing the camera down from his face.

I nodded and didn't look his way. I wasn't sure how much he knew. The downside of a small town is everyone knows everybody else's business. There was no way to hide here, even if you did go to dinner in a different town. Her car was at my place and someone had to have seen it. The reality is, Michael may know the whole story without me ever speaking a word about it.

"It's good. Nothing to worry about," I answered.

He turned towards me.

"We should get back to the office and start. We need to break the story."

I opened the Facebook app on my phone. While the social media site may be out of vogue with the younger generations, it was still vital to the newspaper's success. The town's community page was vibrant and active, and almost everyone turned to the app first thing to find out what was going on in town. If I was going to break the story, it was going to be there.

I started to type and Michael looked over my shoulder. After some edits I finally finished, ready to post. "Breaking: Two gunshot victims found at Bedford Farms this morning. One was taken by ambulance to the health center, before being transferred to DHMC. The other was found dead upon the police's arrival. The state police have taken over the investigation, with the local police assisting. Stay tuned for updates."

I looked over at Michael.

"What do you think?"

He nodded his approval, and I pushed '*post*'. We watched as the blue bar at the top of the page rolled from left to right, before the word '*posted*' popped up.

"We broke the story," I said. "Now the real work begins."

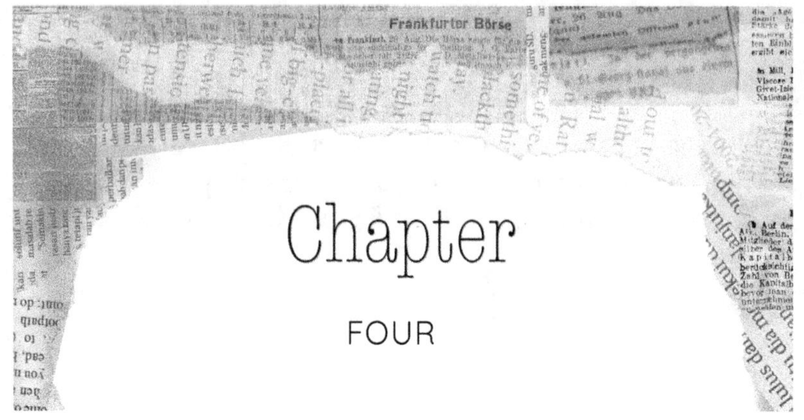

Chapter FOUR

We met back at the office, parking in our usual spots. Michael's had a sign that read, *'Reserved for Editor of The Black River Recorder. All others will be towed'*. The town gifted it to him on his sixtieth birthday.

I got out of my car and stretched. It had already been a long day, and it was barely 8 AM. I needed something to eat and I needed coffee, now. I walked into the office and dumped my backpack next to my desk, before sliding into my chair, and firing up my computer. I have an ancient Mac, named Gertrude, a computer born the same year I started middle school. Even though she had her quirks, she still worked. I also had my personal laptop, which I usually brought to the office with me because the internet was pretty slow on Gertrude.

Michael immediately went over to the coffee pot and started it up. The newspaper ran on coffee and there was almost always a fresh pot. We were going to be here for a while and the only way we'd keep going was with some java. I waited for my computer to warm up—it took her awhile to start—when my office phone rang.

"Alice Fantone, Black River Recorder," I said.

There was silence on the other end of the line.

"Hello?"

"Alice, it's Dickie. You didn't get this from me."

I flipped open a notebook and grabbed a pen, taking the cap off with my teeth.

"Shoot," I said.

Dickie let out a deep sigh on the other end. He had something to tell me, but he wasn't sure.

"Dickie, it won't come back to you. I won't quote you and I'll confirm the information you give me independently of what you tell me. You're good."

"I could get in trouble, but you need to know. The state police just had us pick up Will Ward."

I froze.

"Will Ward?"

"One and the same. They brought him in for questioning as a person of interest. I think it's bullshit, but they seem to think he had something to do with the shooting."

"Thanks, Dickie. If something happens with Will, call me."

He hung up.

I sat back in my chair and undid the bun on top of my head. I ran my fingers through my hair, working the knots out. All the while, my mind rolled the information over.

Will Ward was a local kid who happened to fuck up. *A lot*. He'd been caught driving under the influence and for some petty crimes. He stole some bikes from the front of the library in broad daylight. He ripped off the convenience store. All his crimes were drug related. He had a nasty heroin addiction and had been to rehab three times; the last trip was court mandated. That was almost over a year ago and he'd been out of trouble since.

Will was one of those people who got served a shit hand from the jump. His dad was out of the picture, he had five siblings, and his oldest sister basically raised him. Mrs. Ward was out of work most of the time, due to a nasty cancer diagnosis when Will was still just a kid. So it was up to Marla, his sister, to keep everything running in the family. She did her best, but Will got sucked in by the lure of feeling nothing, like so many others. The siren song of Smack was too much for him and he was addicted for years.

But he was clean now and on the straight and narrow, from what I thought. He had a job at Bedford Farms as a maintenance guy. Otis, the ancient farm manager, hired him right out of rehab and was part of the reason he's stayed sober. Otis takes no shit and makes sure everything is done the right way; there's no cutting corners on his watch. He also loves Will like a son and bailed him out of jail on more than one occasion. When Will got clean, he was more than happy to hire him at the farm.

I had the feeling the state police were barking up the wrong tree. Will had a past, but nothing ever violent. Everything he ever did was to support his habit. He stole to buy drugs. Murder seemed like a pretty big jump from stealing some cash from the gas station for a fix.

"Dickie just called. The cops just brought Will Ward in for questioning," I said to Michael as he handed me a steaming cup of coffee. "Apparently, he's a person of interest."

Michael sat down; his chair groaned. He took a sip of coffee before placing the mug on his desk.

"Really, Will? He doesn't strike me as a murderer. He never even carried a gun when he robbed The Kwik."

Michael was right. Will always committed crime in a

somewhat peaceful way. He literally begged for money from Old Man Murphy down at The Kwick, the local gas station, the last time he did something. He never carried a weapon, just waited for an opportunity, and took it.

"I guess they think he's somehow involved. I don't see it, but I'm curious why they brought him in. Could he have been at the farm?"

Michael tilted his head to one side, thinking.

"Maybe he called 911?"

I shook my head and thought about that.

"There's no way. Will doesn't trust the cops with good reason. He would never help. He might call Otis, but not Dickie."

We sat in silence for a moment, drinking our coffee and thinking. This arrest—or whatever it was—didn't make any sense. It was a stretch that Will would commit a crime as heinous as this one. This was a huge escalation. Did he even have a gun? Most folks around here did, because they were big hunters, but for some reason Will didn't strike me as a firearms owner. Sure, he's committed some crimes, but he always seemed peaceful and remorseful after the fact. I really didn't think he was someone that would do something like murder.

"I don't think it was Will. I also don't think this was just some random act of violence. Whoever did it had to know Nathaniel and Byron would be in that barn early in the morning. I mean, why the hell were they in there anyways?"

Last year, Nathaniel, Byron, and their friends got in trouble with the cops because they were shooting skeet at 6 AM on Thanksgiving morning. Someone called it in to complain about the noise and Dickie went over and broke it up. Supposedly, the boys were drunk and stupid. They never went to bed the night before and decided it was a good idea to shoot off guns. They didn't get in trouble, they were just told to knock it off.

It made perfect sense that nothing happened to them. Nathaniel was the son of the select board chair, owner of the most important business in town, and the grandson of Vermont's junior senator. Byron's dad was the local doctor. Their friends were all protected because those two were protected.

Rumors always swirled about Nathaniel and Byron. I knew they were into drugs, but I didn't know how deep. I'm almost positive the lacrosse camp they went to a few summers ago was a rehab stint, but I couldn't prove it. Plus, it wasn't news per say. It was more information I kept in my back pocket for a rainy day. It seemed today was the day the storm broke.

"I know the boys are into drugs. I can't prove it yet, but I know it," I said breaking the silence. "Was this a drug deal gone bad?"

Michael sighed deeply.

"That's the last thing we need," he said.

A few months before I started at The Recorder, there was a massive drug bust in our town and three others. The state police's drug task force finally lived up to its mission and arrested close to forty people. It made The New York Times. As much as the cops wanted to count this as a win, everyone they arrested was low level or an addict. They didn't get the big fish they hoped for, and drugs were still making their way into Black River.

Vermont might have a bucolic reputation, but it had some serious problems. Education was expensive and not great. There weren't many jobs, especially if you wanted to go to college. Brain drain was real in a place like Black

River. We had Bedford Farms, but all those jobs were blue collar. There was a health clinic, but it was small and didn't attract talent. The other jobs available were all in the hospitality sector, catering to tourists that came up to ski or hike.

Black River was once a gem of Vermont. There used to be a machine tool factory in town, but it had been boarded up for the most part since the late eighties. All those jobs disappeared, and there wasn't something to take up the employment space that had been there before. Black River fell into an economic depression, and it had barely pulled itself out. There was some new development, with the addition of high-speed internet and incentivizing remote workers to move to the area, but it was still a mostly unemployed, blue collar kind of town.

There were still fancy mansions that once held the titans of industry for the machine tool businesses. Most of them sat empty, waiting for some eccentric millionaire to show up and turn them into a bed and breakfast. A few had occupants but only in the summer; their owners went south for the winter. The Black River, where the town gets its name, separates the town into two. On one side, up in the mountains, money—or the appearance of it—ruled. On the other side, everyone was one flu bug away from homelessness.

I fit somewhere in between. I was broke, like everyone else in town, but I had a college degree and a job that required it. I moved willingly to town, where most people my age and educational pedigree moved away the moment they had a chance. I did the same thing with my hometown and ended up here by some twist of fate. I wanted out of Indiana so badly I went to the first spot that would take me; I'd been in Vermont ever since.

I graduated from the University of Notre Dame three

years earlier, with a degree in political science and journalism, plus four years working at a college daily, and two internships at the South Bend Tribune under my belt. I had the experience Michael was looking for even though I was fresh out of college. In some ways, I was still a cub reporter and in others I was as grizzled and jaded as they come. There was so much I hadn't seen or covered, but I was a local politics pro. I'd covered elections, Development Review Board fights, and the opening of a Domino's Pizza that had the town's restaurant owners up in arms.

But this felt like my first *real* story. The first time something really happened in the three years since I rolled into town with nothing more than a notebook and a dream. I wanted out. I wanted to write for a bigger and better newspaper. I wanted to live in a city and have the chance to talk to people my own age. I was ready to move on, and this might just be the story that wrote me out of this town.

"We've got to totally redo the front page. Hell, we've got to scrap the whole paper," Michael said, staring at the screen of his computer with a frown.

"Why don't we just start over? Have you called the printer?"

The Recorder always printed a special Saturday edition of the paper the week of Thanksgiving. Usually, we publish on Friday. There wasn't enough going on—or enough money—to publish daily, so we published once a week instead. Important stories got updated on our website, but most stories had to wait until Friday to be read. Thanksgiving was special because the Friday after the holiday, Christmas season started in Black River. The lighted tractor parade ended with Santa arriving in the town square, where he would sit in the gazebo and hear all the kids' Christmas wishes. People came from the surrounding towns to watch. It was an event with a capital *E*.

We pushed the paper release date to cover it. But this year it might not even happen and if it did, may not make the paper. What was once front-page news would be relegated to page seven, barely a blurb written. This story was the biggest thing to happen in Black River since the drug bust, and this was even bigger than that. Someone died—and it wasn't an accident. Shit happens sometimes in a rural, small town. There's ATV accidents and drownings at the lake, but that's about it. There hasn't been a violent death, well, *ever* in town. At least, not in modern history.

I opened our formatting software and started to rearrange everything I'd already done. Hours of work down the drain but it didn't matter. When something big happens, sometimes that's how it works. All this news wasn't important anymore. Who would care about Gail's Thanksgiving display at the co-op when there's a dead body lying on a slab in the county morgue?

After I deleted everything, I opened a blank document and started to shape my story. I made a list of who I needed to talk to: Marla Ward, the coroner, Sarah, the Bedford and Avery families, Dickie, the chief, and anyone else that might pop up. I needed quotes about the cause of death from the coroner, even though I knew it was a gunshot wound. I needed more from the police, especially about Will's arrest. I had basically nothing to craft a story at this point and I was frustrated. It felt silly sitting here at my desk when I should be out chasing down leads.

I stood up and started to pack notebooks into my backpack and stuck a pen in my bun.

"I'm going out. I need to figure out what's going on and I'm not going to do that here," I said to Michael.

He nodded. "Be careful and keep me updated. Where do you think you'll go?"

"I'm going to the Ward's, back to the scene, maybe The Kwik to get the gossip. If you hear about the press conference, let me know and I'll meet you wherever they hold it."

He nodded again and waved as I walked out of the building.

Chapter

FIVE

I got in my car, sitting for a moment. *Where to?* I didn't have any leads, other than Will. I knew I needed to find out more about what was going on there, but I also knew that going over to the Ward house was like stepping on a minefield.

Marla Ward was not my biggest fan. I've covered all her brother's arrests for his various crimes around town, and she blamed me for his reputation. I was not the one that stole from the gas station and tried to hawk little kid's bikes snatched from the front of the library. I just reported the stories. I did my job. I knew there was no chance in hell she would talk to me, but I had to try. She might have important information.

I pulled out of my parking spot and started the short drive over to the Ward residence. They lived across the river in a ramshackle house that needed a paint job. There was a rusted Jeep in the front yard, with grass growing up into it. The yard was a mess of weeds, children's toys, and metal scraps. The porch sagged with years, like an old woman's face. I parked across the street and took a deep breath. Who knew what I was walking into. Marla could either welcome me in or spit in my face; there was no in between.

I walked over some hot wheels cars and an old bumper towards the porch. My foot was barely on the first step before the door swung open.

"What the fuck do you want, Alice?"

I took another step, one foot on the lower step and one above. But I stopped. I was on perilous ground.

"Marla, I just want to talk and find out what happened this morning. I'm not here to cause problems, I'm here to figure out what's going on."

She narrowed her eyes and took a long drag from her cigarette. She seemed to think for a moment, decide, and then change her mind.

"Get your ass in here, flatlander, before I change my mind."

She moved to let me in, holding the screen door open. I followed her through the door towards the back of the house. We walked into a surprisingly sunny, happy kitchen. From the outside of the house, I figured the inside would look similar. The kitchen was outdated, but scrubbed clean, neat, and orderly. Marla motioned for me to sit at a fifties formica table.

"What do you want?" She asked as she took one more drag of the cigarette, stubbed it out in an ashtray on the table, and then lit another.

"I know the cops picked your brother up and I want to know what happened. I'm here 'cause I want the real story, not rumors."

She sighed and placed her hands on her eyes, careful to keep the burning cigarette away. Marla looked so much older than her twenty-five years. We were the same age, but time hadn't been kind to her. She looked almost two decades older. My dad would describe her as *'rode hard and put away wet.'* I hated that saying, but it was a perfect description of her. She had lines around her mouth from years of smoking, and her hair was stringy with no luster. Marla was far too skinny, all sharp angles and edges. Her eyes were cold with a deep exhaustion that could only come from a life lived hard. She'd taken on too much too soon and it showed.

"Those fuckers came and demanded to come in. I told them not without a warrant, but Will's a dumbass and went with them, even though he don't trust cops."

I flipped open a notebook and wrote everything down.

"Why did he go?"

She sighed and let out a long stream of smoke. Her breath control was insane, like an opera singer's, which was impressive considering her nicotine habit.

"He kept saying he didn't know what they were talkin' about. They finally told us what it was about the shootin'. He said he had nothin' to hide." she said. "They're gonna try and pin this on him. I know it. He's been here all night and all this mornin'. We woke up early to get started on food. But they wouldn't listen to me."

"Did they take him out in cuffs?"

She shook her head *no*, and took another drag.

"No, but they threw him in the back of a cruiser. They made him look guilty. He has an alibi, but they won't listen to a fuckin' word I said."

Just then, one of the younger kids ran into the room. They had on footie pajamas and had a juice box in their hand. There was peanut butter on their cheek, most likely leftover from breakfast.

"Marla, can I have Goldfish?"

Their voice was soft. This kid hadn't been beaten down

by life yet, was still full of hope and love. They were the direct opposite of Marla. But she lit up when her younger sibling asked for some crackers. It was like years melted off her face. She obviously loved her siblings and lived for them.

"Of course, baby. Get 'em from the cabinet. Just don't eat the whole bag."

As the kiddo walked by, she ran her hand over their head lovingly. We both sat in silence while the little kid grabbed their snack. As they left, she turned back to me.

"Alice, I'm tellin' you, he didn't do it. Hell, we were barely up and drinkin' coffee when it probably happened. He was with me all mornin' till they came and took him."

I nodded, still writing in my notebook.

"I believe you; I really do. I'm not sure why they took him in, but I'm guessing they think this shooting is somehow related to drugs," I said.

"He's clean! He's been clean for a year!"

I put my hands up.

"I know. I'm not saying he isn't. I just don't think the state police believe him. And they're looking for a scapegoat —he's an easy mark because of his past."

She nodded and tears welled in her eyes. One fell and slid down her cheek. She didn't brush it away.

"You know they made Dickie do it? Come and pick him up. He didn't want to, but they made him."

That's why Dickie called me. He was the one to do it, against his will. He knew Will didn't do this, but who was going to listen to a small-town police deputy? Especially Dickie. He was a bit of a caricature of what a cop should be. He wore his pants too high up on his waist and they were so short you could always see his tube socks. He wanted nothing more than to become a cop when he grew up but couldn't ever pass the physical exam because of his asthma. On his final chance, he finished the mile run with just seconds to go and finally made his dream come true. But he had to take two weeks off because he got shin splints so bad he couldn't walk.

Dickie's not a bad guy and he wouldn't do something like bring Will in unless he had some kind of evidence. The state police were just going off history, not fact. I knew in my gut that Will had nothing to do with this. He was clean. He'd gone straight. And he'd never done anything that was remotely close to murder, so why start now, when his life was finally back on track?

"Those fuckers better let him go. If they arrest him, I'm rainin' hell down on 'em."

I looked over at Marla and studied her for a moment. She sat in a cloud of silvery smoke, her eyes hard and her mouth in a firm line. She wasn't someone that took bull-shit and what she just said wasn't a threat; it was a promise.

"You need to get a lawyer. Call legal aid and see if you can get someone to get to the station for him. He's going to cooperate, and they're going to try and say this was him."

She nodded.

"We don't have money for any lawyer, but I'll figure it out."

I stood and started to walk back towards the door but stopped in the doorway to the hallway.

"Marla, I'm going to report the facts. If Will was involved, and I'm only saying *if*, I'll write about it. If the cops took him in with no proof and just history, I'll cover it. I can't promise you what I'll end up writing, but I do promise you it will be the truth."

She nodded once and I left.

AS I PICKED my way across the Ward's yard, I thought about what Marla told me. Will had an alibi, he was with her. But they still wanted to talk to him. If the police weren't looking at him as a suspect, why bring him in? If they just wanted to talk to him, to see what he might know, why didn't they talk to him at home? They must be thinking the same thing I am. *This is about drugs.* So far, no one's been able to stop the source. And while Will may be intimately familiar with the dealers in town, I didn't see him flipping on anyone. He's not going to rat out someone who could potentially come after him and his family. Plus, he's not like that. Will wouldn't snitch.

Dickie and the chief had to know that. All the times he got arrested, he never told them who and where he got the drugs from. Even with the promise of less probation or jail time, he never said a word. He lived by a code and one of the tenets was to keep your mouth shut.

I didn't know where to go next. I could try to go back to the scene, and see what's going on, or I could head to The Kwik, our local gas station. I checked my phone for messages, just to make sure I didn't miss anything from Michael. There was nothing and for a moment, I sat in the driver's seat, just staring into space. I'd seen a dead body this morning. I'd seen a person that could very well be on their way to becoming a dead body. It was more than I could handle, the image of Byron on the concrete floor of the barn, his left shoe blown off his foot. He was just so still. The image of him lying there was stuck in my mind and filled me with anxiety. My palms got sweaty, and I could feel the bile rise in my throat. I opened the car door just in time to puke up all the coffee I drank earlier.

I slid to the side of my seat and let my head hang between my knees for what felt like years. I couldn't sit up because each time I did, I dry heaved. I'd seen a dead body, and I wasn't handling it very well. I had to pull my shit together. I couldn't report this story if I kept puking. Shakily I sat up and let the uneasy feeling roll over me, taking deep breaths and trying not to think about Byron Avery and his missing shoe. Once I felt like I wasn't going to hurl if I moved, I leaned back into my seat and closed the door. I rest my cheek against the cold glass and it felt marvelous. I gave myself to the count of ten to sit there, and then put the key in the ignition and drove.

I PULLED into The Kwik a few minutes later. I needed water to swish in my mouth, and weirdly, I needed a cup of coffee with a vengeance. When I walked in, Old Man Murphy waved from behind the counter. He's owned the gas station, affectionately known as The Kwik, for decades. I come in just about every day for a coffee or something else, and he was the first person in town I could count as a friend. Old Man Murphy takes care of me. Every morning, he saves me hash browns and a breakfast biscuit. I mentioned in passing once that I liked hazelnut coffee, he brews it every day now. The Kwik is my home away from home, the place I go when I need a pick me up, either in the form of a coffee or a pep talk from the proprietor.

"Alice, how goes it? You been at Bedford's?" Old Man Murphy said as I walked in the door.

I nodded. "I got there not too far behind the cops. And now I'm out chasing leads."

He walked around the counter and poured me a cup of

coffee. He didn't put it in a paper cup, rather a mug that read 'World's Best Grandpa.' He handed me the cup.

"What else do you need? You eaten yet? You're gonna need to fuel up to last the day."

He walked over to the little oven thing that keeps food warm and grabbed two biscuits and hash browns. I put my coffee down on the counter.

"I'll be in the bathroom, real quick."

Old Man Murphy nodded and motioned towards the bathroom, as if shooing me in that direction. After I locked the door, I leaned against it and took a steadying breath. I didn't want to admit it, but I was a wreck. My hands were still shaky, my palms were sweaty. I took a swig of water from the tap, swished it around my mouth, and spit it out into the sink. I felt a little better now that the bile was leaving my mouth. I checked my reflection in the mirror. My hair was frizzed out everywhere and my bun was falling to one side. I quickly washed my face with some cold water, rinsed my mouth out one more time, and redid my hair. That was as good as it was going to get.

I met Old Man Murphy in the back of the store, at the tables where the old guys always drink coffee and gossip. He'd brought my breakfast and coffee back there and as usual, the usual crew was already seated. My plate was next to Lyle and across from Mr. Hancock and his son RJ. All three worked at Bedford Farms before they retired; Mr. Hancock is actually who came up with the recipe for the strawberry rhubarb ice cream. He's in his nineties now, but still sharp as ever.

"Alice, how goes the fourth estate?" Lyle said as I slid into my chair.

"It's been a day, that's for sure."

I took a sip of my coffee and a bite of a fluffy biscuit. I

chewed carefully, afraid I might barf again, but nothing happened. I took that as a good sign and ate some hash browns.

"So, someone really got shot at Bedford's?" Mr. Hancock looked at me through his thick glasses, waiting for my reply. His glasses were so strong they made his eyes magnified.

"Two victims. I can't release the names yet though. One died at the scene and the other is at DHMC."

The men were silent for a moment. RJ fiddled with one of those red straws that you use to stir coffee, and Lyle tapped his fingers against the table. Mr. Hancock just sat there, thinking. I ate more of my biscuit and waited for one of them to talk. If I've learned anything as a journalist, it's the importance of silence. Sometimes the best questions aren't the ones you ask, but the ones that just get answered. Lyle broke first.

"It's gotta be drugs. It don't make sense."

RJ nodded, agreeing with his assessment.

"Did they get the shooter?" Mr. Hancock asked.

"Not that I know. There wasn't anyone at the scene when we arrived and I left when the state police showed up to collect evidence."

The men sat in thoughtful silence as I ate the rest of my breakfast. Old Man Murphy walked back from the front with two coffee pots—I knew one held my favorite.

"It's a shame, really. And on a holiday too. There's two families not having a good start to the season," he said as he topped off all our cups.

"Could someone get to the barns via the woods?" I asked the men. If anyone knew, it would be this crew. They'd spent something like 120 years collectively at

Bedford Farms and knew the place like the back of their hands.

Lyle scratched his head through his beanie and scrunched up his nose.

"I mean, they could, but they'd have to get over the river and it's not frozen over yet. Getting through that cold would slow 'em down. Plus, the river drops off at that section. They might've had to swim."

Mr. Hancock nodded his agreement.

"It wouldn't be easy, and it would've taken time. Whoever did it probably drove away."

I thought about what the men said. I'd toyed with the idea that the shooter ran away through the woods, but I knew eventually they'd hit the river, a natural barrier. Someone would've seen or heard a car if it drove up. There had to be a camera somewhere that caught something.

"Are there cameras on the outside of the barn?" I asked.

RJ shook his head no.

"There are cameras inside, but only in the birthing stalls, to check on the cows at night, nothin' outside. There's a camera on the back door of the shop, but that's it."

No way to escape through the woods and no cameras to catch someone in the act. In many ways, the barn was the perfect spot to shoot someone. But how did they get away? Whoever did this must know something about Bedford Farms. That didn't narrow the suspect pool much though. Nearly the whole town worked there or spent their Saturdays at the farmers' market in the summer. I always thought it wasn't a place that held many secrets, but maybe I was wrong.

"I wonder if Bedford's heard anything from the house?" RJ asked. "They must've heard somethin'."

I thought the same thing all morning. Mrs. Bedford

didn't come outside until the ambulance arrived. The cops arrived before and when Jack pulled up, I doubt he had on the lights and sirens. Why didn't Dickie and the chief arriving draw them out? And why didn't Mr. Bedford come down to the barn with his wife? I had so many questions and wasn't quite sure which to ask.

"I doubt it, you know how he drinks," Lyle said.

All three men shared a knowing glance. I'd heard the rumors that Bobby was a stone-cold alcoholic. He kept his shit together during the day but at night he was a martini fueled menace. How he kept up appearances during the day and got blackout, rip-roaring drunk each night was beyond me.

"You think he was passed out?"

I let the question hang in the air. All three tensed up. I knew they had loyalty to the place. Bedford Farms kept their lights on and food on their table for decades. RJ just retired at the end of the summer. If anyone knew that place's secrets, it would be them. Mr. Hancock itched his head through the bright orange hunting beanie on his head.

"Alice, you didn't hear this from us, but of course that man was dead to the world. He drinks a fifth of vodka every night. How he's not in worse shape is beyond me, but he's a drunk and a mean one at that."

I didn't say anything but filed it all away. So, it was true. Mr. Bedford wasn't the proud son of Black River that he played during public events. I wanted more.

"How do you know?" I asked before popping the last of my biscuit in my mouth.

Again, they shared that look and Lyle cleared his throat.

"Alice, I don't gossip, but let's just say it's something we've all seen with our own eyes. It's not somethin' we're makin' up. It's not just rumor, it's fact."

"Was he ever violent?"

RJ shook his head.

"I know what you're thinkin', but it's not like that, Alice. He wouldn't shoot his kid," he said.

I didn't think so either, but it was worth asking. The Bedford's had something to do with this; I had a feeling it had to do with whatever secrets that farmhouse held. It was as pretty as a postcard from the outside, but the inside sounded like a hellscape of addiction and stress. No wonder Nathaniel allegedly did drugs. If my dad was a crazed alcoholic, I'd probably do the same thing. My dad is soft-spoken and prays the rosary during Notre Dame games.

I had a feeling in my gut I needed to get back to the scene. There were untold secrets here and I needed to uncover them. I finished off my coffee and stood.

"Gentlemen," I said, and saluted them.

Lyle smiled and Mr. Hancock laughed.

I turned to walk away when I heard RJ.

"You be careful out there, Alice. It's not what it seems."

I looked at him, nodded, and headed out of the store. I had a story to write.

Chapter SIX

Not much later, I pulled down the drive of Bedford Farms. There were still cop cars and officers milling about. The plastic sheeting was blocking the barn door, so there was no way I could get in there. I pulled up away from all the state police cruisers and walked over. The gravel and frozen snow crunched under my boots. Two police officers turned when they heard me walking.

"Good morning!" I said, my voice cheery. I did not feel cheery, but I needed to suck up to them.

They both looked at me warily. I mean, they didn't know me and what business I had to be at an active crime scene. I stretched out my hand towards the first guy. He wore glasses and was clean shaven. He couldn't be more than 21.

"Alice Fantone, Black River Recorder," I said, shaking his hand.

"Aiden Walker," he replied.

I shook the other guy's hand, but he didn't say anything, choosing instead to look at me cautiously. He looked a little older and obviously didn't trust me. He was a non-starter, but maybe I could get something out of Aiden.

"How's the investigation going, gentlemen?" I asked, sweetly.

"You don't gotta say shit to her," the other officer said gruffly.

"This is just a friendly conversation," I said. "Completely off the record. Just some background."

He looked at me with steely eyes, his jaw moving, chewing on a toothpick. A smoker if I've ever seen one. My grandpa used to do the same thing. And at the rate he was chewing, he wasn't happy. Aiden looked over at him.

"I mean, we don't know much," he said, shrugging at the other cop. He rolled his eyes and walked away.

"What do you know, Aiden?" I asked.

He scratched his head near his ear. Those police hats with the strap along the back had to be uncomfortable. And I'm guessing he hasn't been in uniform long, so he's probably not used to how it feels yet.

"Not much. There's not much evidence, other than shell casings left, but the team is looking for trace evidence, just in case there's something there," he said.

"That can't be easy in a barn."

He nodded.

"Yes ma'am. We did arrest a suspect."

I froze. *Arrest a suspect?* I was told that Will was brought in for questioning. Not that he was arrested. I couldn't play my hand. I had to let him think I didn't know anything.

"A suspect? Any chance you could let me know who?" I smiled, looking up at him. He smiled back and looked a little flustered. I'm glad to know I can still lay it on thick when I need to, even though I would rather kiss a toad than a man.

"You know I can't tell you that, but I can tell you he's a player in the local drug scene."

Now it was my turn to nod. A local player? I mean, Will could best be described as a local addict, not someone who was actually *in* the game. He had problems, but had never been charged with anything but possession, not even possession with intent to sell. This guy probably didn't know that though.

"Really? So, you think this is a drug related crime?"

I was waiting for his response when I heard my name.

"Alice, don't speak with my officers. Aiden, you can leave."

It was Sarah and she walked towards me. The cranky smoker was next to her, who walked away with Aiden. He turned around and looked back at me, I gave him a smile and a wave.

"Alice," Sarah said, her tone warning.

"It was all off the record, just background," I replied.

She looked at me through narrowed eyes. I put my hands up in surrender.

"I didn't even have a notebook out to write anything down. Honest. Completely off the record. It was just a conversation."

She didn't believe me. I knew it. But how else was I supposed to get information? She couldn't blame me for being industrious.

"Alice, we're having a press conference later today. I recommend you save your questions for then."

Her cheeks were pink from the cold, and they made her blue eyes pop. I wished we were meeting under better circumstances, because I really just wanted to pull her to me and make out. But that's not professional, especially not at the scene of a murder.

"I wouldn't be doing my job if I wasn't sniffing around, Sarah."

She rolled her eyes; I could tell she was trying not to smile.

"I know you're doing your job, and I'm doing mine. Don't talk to my officers."

She turned to walk away from me, but I stopped her in her tracks.

"So, Will Ward is a suspect?"

The stillness in her body was absolute. She didn't move a muscle for a beat, then another, before turning and walking back towards me. The mischief was out of her eyes and they were narrowed in my direction.

"How did you... I'm gonna kill Aiden," she said.

I reached out and touched her arm.

"I got it from somewhere else, he didn't spill anything important," I said. "But really, when did Will move from coming in to talk, to arrested suspect?"

Sarah looked annoyed. She knew I had her. But would she answer me?

"This is off the record. *Completely off.* I will kill you if this ends up in quotes."

I nodded. I was hopefully about to get something good.

"Will Ward was brought in to speak with officers and has since been arrested in connection to crimes surrounding the shooting," she said.

Still, it didn't make sense. Why was he arrested? What did Will do other than be a local fuck-up?

"All due respect, Sarah, but that's bullshit, and you know it."

She looked around, as if to see if we were being

watched. She grabbed my wrist and pulled me further away from the other officers and commotion of the crime scene.

"It's drugs, Alice. That's why they arrested him. The Lieutenant is sure he's involved somehow."

I still couldn't believe it. Will was clean. He was figuring his life out. He was cooking Thanksgiving dinner with his sister just a few hours ago. I really doubted he would throw away everything to go back into the hell-hole that is addiction.

"Drugs? And what does Will have to do with that?"

She looked around again. Sarah was nervous to be seen with me, that was sure.

"Sarah, you're the information officer. You would obviously be the one to speak with me."

She was tense, her body rigid. I knew she wanted to keep rumors at bay, even though we were barely a thing, but this was ridiculous. We were *working*. She is the contact for any information regarding the shooting. Of course we would be together.

"Alice...I swear," she said, pushing her hand into her hair. It made a little bit fall towards her face. I had to fight the urge to push it behind her ear.

"The connection, in my opinion, is tenuous at best. I think they want to say they have the killer, so the community doesn't go ape shit. You cannot print anything I just told you."

My mind was reeling. Nothing made sense. They were going to pin this on an innocent man.

"Why did you tell me?"

She pushed her hand in her hair again, obviously stressed.

"Because, you're right. It's bullshit. Somebody needs to figure out the truth. And that somebody might be you."

I looked at her for a long minute. She didn't have faith in the team she worked with, but she had some weird faith in me. I knew in my bones Will didn't do this. The question was, who did? I reached forward and pushed that loose strand of hair behind her ear. She blushed. I turned to walk back towards my car, but stopped when I heard her call my name. She walked towards me.

"When this is all over, we should get coffee or dinner, something."

She said this sheepishly, as if she knew what she was doing was wrong, but she still wanted to do it.

"Not worried about the guys anymore?"

She dropped her head and gazed at the ground while she spoke.

"I like you. Being around you...it made me realized how much I want to kiss you again. How much I want to hold your hand." She lifted her head and met my gaze. "Fuck them. I'll do what I want in my life."

She reached out, squeezed my hand, turned on her heel and left.

Chapter

SEVEN

I watched Sarah walk away, shocked. One minute, she was telling me about a murder suspect and the next she was asking me out. Talk about whiplash. I didn't know how to handle what just happened, so I did what I did best; compartmentalized. I had a story to write and apparently a crime to solve.

If the cops thought this was drug related, there had to be some truth there; we did have a problem in town. Not as bad as other places, but it was enough of an issue to be covered in the paper monthly. The question I had was, *who was providing the stuff?* If Byron and Nathaniel were high or it was a drug deal gone bad, I'd need to figure out who was behind the sale. Easier said than done.

I wasn't going to solve a crime just standing in a driveway, but I was still at Bedford Farms, so I might as well see if anyone was in the homestead. I made sure no one was paying attention to me before I started to walk over. The house was one of those old Vermont farmhouses that looked like a postcard, even during stick season. It was decorated with seasonal mums and gourds, lining the steps.

I climbed the steps, my boots landing heavy on each one. As I made my way to the door to knock, it swung open. Bobby Bedford stood in front of me.

"Of course it's you," he said, anger flashing in his eyes.

"I'm here seeing if you had anything to say about the shooting this morning."

He stood in a perfectly pressed pair of jeans, with a Patagonia quarter zip with the Bedford Farm logo on one side. He looked fancy—Vermont fancy—but still completely put together. Much more together than I probably looked. We just stared at each other until I heard the clink of ice cubes in a glass. Bobby swirled the tumbler in his hand. It was full of clear liquid with a wedge of lime. Vodka already?

"Alice, I don't have to tell you anything. You want me to tell you some fucking sob story, something heartwarming for your little shit rag paper? Here's the truth. My son is a fuck up that had access to too much money and no boundaries. He had cash to burn, that dumbass decided to spend it on pills. How's that for your story?"

I just stood there. He said the quiet part out loud.

"Do you know how he got his hands on the drugs?"

He laughed and took a long swig from his glass.

"How the fuck do I know? If we knew, maybe he wouldn't be in emergency surgery right now with a bullet hole in his chest."

He took another drink, my hand was itching to pull out a notebook, but that didn't seem to be the right move. I needed something I could print, and I doubted that the rambling of an obviously drunk, grieving father counted. I mean, if this was what grieving looked like.

"Do you have an update on Nathaniel?"

Bobby rolled his eyes and leaned against the door frame. He looked like one of those models in the Kohls catalog we used to get when I was growing up. Handsome in a generic way that would make someone want to buy chinos. I realized that there was nothing special about Bobby. He was a cookie-cutter wealthy Vermonter. Still in outdoor gear, but the expensive kind.

"There's no update. I don't know if he's alive or dead. My wife hasn't told me and frankly, I don't care. If he dies then it's his own damn fault."

Shit. Bobby was heartless. His kid was found bleeding out just a few hours ago and rushed to a hospital almost an hour away for emergency surgery, and he gave two fucks. What was Bobby's issue?

"Why do you say it was his fault?"

He sneered.

"Alice, we've spent thousands trying to get his ass clean. Each time, he'd come back here and we'd start over. Even when he was at Andover, he was still using. It was flushing money down the toilet—he got what was coming."

Bobby took another drink and gestured with his glass, spilling a little onto the floor.

"Let me tell you something, life's about choices. And my only son chose wrong. It's not my problem anymore. Regardless of what happens, he's dead to me."

Bobby straightened and I turned to see a black Audi drive up and park. Out walked the Senator, Bobby's dad. Robert Bedford is the patriarch of the Bedford family. He's also a political powerhouse in our small state. He won Patrick Leahy's seat in the Senate when he retired but was the President Pro Tempore of the Vermont State Senate before that. He's known for whipping votes and getting exactly what he wants. His opinion will either kill a bill or let it live to see another day.

"Alice, how lovely," he said, his gaze stony.

I was the last person he wanted to see. I snuck a look at Bobby, and I was pretty sure he wanted to see his dad about as much as he wanted to see the inside of a woodchipper.

"Bobby, go inside before you embarrass yourself more," he said, his voice cold.

Bobby opened his mouth to argue but the Senator shot him a look, he went back into the house, closing the door. He turned his attention to me. He stood at the bottom of the steps and I was at the top, making us almost the same height. I'm short and the Senator is tall, an imposing figure on a good day and a terrifying one right now. The man was not happy to see me talking to his son.

"Alice, I will tell you this once and once only. Everything you heard here is off the record. If I see even a drop of ink lay out what was spoken here, I will sue the paper for defamation. Michael doesn't have the funds for a lawyer, and I will bury you both. If you ever want a career of more than whatever it is you do now, you will keep your mouth shut and not write a damn word you heard here. Are we clear?"

I didn't want to be intimidated, but I was. I felt like I was going to vomit again. The Senator didn't play. If anyone could ruin my life, it would be him. He has connections all over the country—if I wanted a job somewhere else, he could keep it from happening. And I had no doubt he would sue me. I make fifteen bucks an hour; lawyer money is not something I have. I may have been shaking, but I held my chin up high. I looked him in the eye.

"Afraid of the family dirty laundry being aired out, Senator?"

I've never been hit in the face, but there was a moment I thought the man was going to reach out and deck me. Fury rolled over him before a scary calm settled once again across his face. The Senator was not someone who people back-talked. And I just did.

"You'll need to have something worth printing to scare me, Alice. You have nothing and you know it."

He walked up the stairs past me and headed to the door. He was right, everything Bobby said wasn't anything I could print. Or even would print. But it gave me background, gave me more information than I had earlier in the day. The Bedford family was obviously a mess; Nathaniel was the center of the chaos. I started to walk down the stairs, but the Senator's voice stopped me. I turned around.

"Just remember, little girl, this was all off the record. I can—and will—end you if need be."

He opened the door and walked into the house. I stood for a moment before I walked back across the driveway, towards my car. My thoughts were swirling with what just happened. I needed to get information to corroborate what Bobby said without using anything he told me.

When I got to my car, I slipped behind the wheel and sat for a moment. I wasn't sure of my next move, but I had an idea. It was a risk, but one worth taking. I put the key in the ignition, backed up, and drove away, following my hunch.

Chapter EIGHT

I got back to the office and headed straight to my desk. Michael came out of the small kitchen off the back of our office, which was really just one large room, with a separate enclosed office for him, a desk for me, and another desk with the computer we did layout on.

"Catch anything good?"

I turned on my computer and shedded my coat. I sat down before answering.

"I mean, yes and no. Bobby Bedford said some shit, but the Senator came up and threatened to sue if we published any of it. And Will Ward was originally taken into the station to have a conversation, and he has since then been arrested."

Michael nodded and took a sip of his coffee.

"Where did you get all of this?"

I sighed and pulled my long hair out of my bun, before sweeping it back up.

"I have Marla Ward on the record, and I've got an idea to corroborate some of what Bobby said but in a way that the Senator can't sue us for all we're worth. And the rest is from Sarah, but not for print."

Michael sat down gingerly, protecting his back. He had a skiing accident when he was younger and his back flares up when it gets cold. Basically, it hurts him for half the year. He took his glasses off, set them down gently, and rubbed his eyes.

"So right now, we don't have much."

I nodded. He was right, I had next to nothing. I had information, but I couldn't use it, which is the worst. I needed to get someone on the record. And I had an idea of who I could. I grabbed my phone and opened Instagram. A quick search led me to Nathanial Bedford's page, where a picture from last year's spring break had a few boys from town tagged. Andrew Porter, Colin Hutson, and John Carter all lived locally. I looked up some addresses in the town phone book and scribbled them down on the back of a receipt.

"I've got an idea," I said to Michael, as I put on my coat. "It might amount to nothing, but it might give us what we need."

He nodded and took another sip of coffee.

"I'm reworking the paper and I've already called the printer. We have a deadline of ten tonight. When you get me a chance, send me pictures from earlier."

I stopped what I was doing and opened my photos app, uploading all the photos I took earlier to our Dropbox. After waiting for all the pictures to transfer, I slipped my phone in my pocket and made sure I had my car keys.

"You've got photos. Call me if you hear about a press conference. Sarah said there's gonna be one but never gave me a time."

Michael waved as I walked out the door.

THE HOUSE WAS massive and on the outskirts of town, in the opposite direction of Bedford Farms. This farm was for horses—Hutson and Sons—home of Colin, friend of Nathaniel and Byron. I rolled down the long driveway and took in the horses in the fenced-in pasture. They were standing, watching me, as if they were sentries protecting the farm. Similar to Bedford's, there was a fork in the drive; the right side led to the barns and the left towards the house.

Where the Bedford's house was colonial, this one was a modern log cabin, with large windows and a wrap-around porch. I stopped and took a moment before getting out of my car. I wasn't just about to cold-call someone, I was about to burst into their Thanksgiving Day and ask about drugs. There was a very real chance I was about to get kicked out of this house before I ever got invited in.

When I got to the front door, I was about to knock when it opened. A short, pretty, blonde woman stood before me in a pair of Christmas pajamas and a turkey apron.

"Hi. My name is Alice Fantone, I'm the reporter at The Black River Recorder."

I put out my hand to shake it and she grabbed it warmly.

"Of course, I know who you are, Alice! What brings you here on Thanksgiving?" She said.

I swallowed and took a breath before asking. It just occurred to me that they may not know what happened this morning. By this time, I thought the whole town would know, but the news may not have reached the Hutson household.

"I'm here to speak with your son, Colin, about Nathaniel Bedford and Byron Avery. Is that okay?"

Her face fell and she shook her head.

"It's so awful what happened this morning. We heard on the police scanner and Mrs. Bedford called not to long after. I just hope they're okay."

So, she knew what happened, but maybe wasn't aware anyone was dead. I wasn't about to share that information. It wasn't lying by not telling them, just omitting the truth. Kind of the same thing, but I didn't need them to clam up because someone died. I needed information and I figured at least one of Byron and Nathaniel's friends would talk.

"I do too. May I speak with Colin? I need some information about the boys. You can totally sit in with him during the interview."

She motioned for me to come in and closed the door behind me. I slipped out of my wet boots and put them on the boot tray next to the door before following Mrs. Hutson into her home, presumably towards the kitchen. The room was light and airy, with light wood and green accents. In a large breakfast nook, Colin Hutson sat in work clothes, eating French toast.

"Mom, who is it?" He said, through a full mouth.

"Colin, this is Alice. She's from the paper and has some questions."

He looked confused for a moment and shoveled more French toast in his mouth. He had pink cheeks and must've come in from barn chores not long ago. Mrs. Hutson motioned for me to sit down next to Colin and busied herself around the kitchen, placing a cup of coffee and a little pitcher of cream in front of me.

"Why do you want to talk to me?" He asked.

"Well, I'm looking for some information about Nathaniel and Byron. You're all friends?"

He nodded. His expression was wary, but open. It was

like he wasn't quite sure what to do, but at the same time curious about what I wanted. I needed to play this right. I had to get Colin talking and I hoped he would be honest with his mom around.

"Do you both mind if I record this? We'll be on the record, Colin, which means I can print what you say."

He shifted nervously in his seat.

"You'll print what I say?"

I nodded. "I might not use direct quotes from you, depending on the way the story goes, but you'll be helping me fill in some holes that I've got questions about. If you would like to remain anonymous, I can protect your identity. The only person who would know it was you would be my editor, Michael. It's up to you."

He looked over at his mom, who nodded. When he looked back at me, he took a deep breath, before taking a long sip of milk. When he placed the cup down, he had a milk mustache and didn't look like the teenager he was, but more like the child he used to be.

"Can I tell you if I want to be anonymous after we talk?"

I smiled. I might actually get something out of him. I had to be gentle, but this idea may pan out.

"Absolutely, I'll do whatever makes you comfortable."

I put my phone on the table and opened my recording app. I flipped my notebook to a fresh page and clicked my pen. I was ready for him, but was he ready for me?

"Will you state your name and spell it for me?" I said, as I turned on the recorder.

He leaned towards the phone and, a little too loudly, said his name and spelled it out.

"You can talk normally, it'll pick up."

His mom walked over and placed a plate of fudge in

front of us. She winked at me. I was about to ask her son about a violent crime, and she was plying me with homemade sweets. I was living in some weird alternate universe where nothing went wrong this morning. And I was about to burst their bubble.

"Do you know what happened this morning at Bedford Farm?"

Colin looked down at his hands.

"Byron and Nate got shot."

He did know. At least I wasn't going to have to explain what happened. I wasn't about to mention the fact that Byron was dead. It wasn't my information to share. It felt bad keeping it from him, but I was under a gag order from the cops. Plus, I needed him to focus on the information I needed. Not grief of finding out his friend was dead. It felt a little heartless, but it was my reality right now.

"I have some questions about them. And they may not be easy to answer, but I want you to tell me honestly what you know. If you don't know something, that's okay. Just be honest, can you do that?"

He looked up at his mom, who was leaning against the counter, her face somewhat concerned. She nodded in his direction, a silent seal of approval.

"How long have you known Byron and Nathaniel?"

He swallowed and clasped his hands in his lap.

"Since we were kids, for as long as I can remember. They go to Andover now and I'm in school here, but we're still friends."

I wrote in my notebook.

"This might not be an easy question to answer, but there's some rumors swirling, and I'm just trying to get the facts straight. Did one or both of them have some issues with drugs?"

Colin looked towards his mom and then down at his hands.

"You're not going to get in trouble however you answer," I said gently. "I'm trying to piece together what happened today and there's a rumor it may have involved drugs."

He took a shaky breath and nodded.

"I mean, Nate had a problem. Bryon liked to smoke, and he'd do anything Nate did. But he wasn't like Nate."

I made a note.

"What do you mean?"

And that's when the floodgates opened. Colin sighed and spilled everything.

"It started summer before freshman year. He was going to Andover in the fall and started to party really hard. I still hung out with them, but I've never been into that stuff. It just got worse as we got older. He could get pills easily at school, but it was harder when he was home. Then all of a sudden, this summer, he was always high."

Even though I was recording, I wrote down every word. I didn't want to miss anything. Now I had proof that there were drugs involved. I just needed to know where they were coming from.

"And do you know where the pills came from?"

He shook his head.

"He got secretive. I mean, he would do stuff, but only when partying. But then he started even when he wasn't partying. He said he had a way to get it, so he might as well."

He started out like so many rich kids—with parties and ended up doing so many drugs that he was found almost dead on a cold barn floor. Colin confirmed he had a local dealer, but who was it?

"Do you know Will Ward?" I asked.

Colin looked down at his hands. He was nervous again. My stomach dropped.

"I mean, we know Will, but he's older than us. Bryon used to have him buy weed from the dispensary in Windsor, but that was it. Will's been sober since he got out of rehab. He wouldn't buy for Byron anymore."

They knew Will and used him for his ID to buy legal weed. He could've been Nathaniel's hook up, but everyone made it seem like he was truly out of the game. I couldn't see him risking it all.

"Did Nathaniel and Bryon ever use with Will?"

He shook his head again.

"Will always did hard stuff. Nate and Byron weren't into that, at least I don't think so."

Mrs. Hutson came over and cleared her son's dishes. She leaned over and kissed him on the head, a very mom-like move.

"Nate and Byron are good boys, but they've taken a bit of a wrong path. They needed more structure than they're given," she said. "They needed some parenting, not to be sent off to boarding school."

Obviously, Mrs. Hutson wasn't into the parenting style of the Bedford or Avery families. She did have a point. Her kid was doing barn chores and eating French toast in her kitchen, completely safe, while the other two were either in an operating room or a slab in the coroner's office. Sure, her kid didn't go to a fancy boarding school, but he also didn't have a drug problem.

"When you say Nate got secretive over the summer, what do you mean?"

He put his hands in his lap and looked down, before looking back up at me.

"He kept driving somewhere and wouldn't let us go

with him. We'd be out doing something, and he'd just leave but come back kinda quickly. He never said where and if we'd ask, he'd get weird, so I just stopped asking. He always came back with more stuff though."

I scribbled more in my notebook.

"When you say stuff, you mean pills?"

Colin nodded.

"And he wasn't taking too long to get back when he'd leave?"

He nodded again. So, Nathaniel's source was local. I knew heroin moved through the area, but who was selling pills? Most of the time people couldn't get their hands on them so they turned to the harder stuff. But it seemed he never made that move. Will used to be into the hard stuff, while Nathaniel was snorting pills. Whoever he was buying from had to have some sort of unlimited source. Pills were harder to get now, and we lived in Vermont, there weren't pain clinics on every corner like in Florida. Those kind of operations were all basically shutdown now that everyone knows how addictive Oxy and the like are.

"Colin, is there anything else you want to add?"

He looked at me for a moment and then his gaze shifted over my head. He had a look on his face like he was deep in thought.

"Nate and Byron got really messed up. It was pills all the time and not like we used to be. I haven't spent much time with them 'cause I'm not into that."

He sighed and his face fell. He obviously cared about Byron and Nate, but they moved apart.

"I saw you all went on spring break last year?"

He nodded and kept looking at his hands.

"It was the last time we really hung out. Nate was sober.

It was like it used to be. But by the time he got back for summer, it was all fucked up again."

Mrs. Hutson clicked her tongue, obviously not happy with her son's language.

"Sorry Mom," he said, his cheeks reddening.

I turned off my recorder and closed my notebook. I'd taken enough of Colin's time and got the information I needed. There was a drug problem between both of them. Now, it was my job to figure out where the drugs were coming from. I stood up to leave, my coffee untouched, but stopped myself before I left the kitchen.

"Do you know why Nathaniel and Byron would be in the barn this morning?"

Colin shrugged.

"They always had a party the night before Thanksgiving. I went over there for a little bit last night, but I left. They were already messed up."

I smiled at him and nodded at Mrs. Hutson.

"Thank you both. I really appreciate it," I said.

With that, I saw myself out.

Chapter
NINE

As I got into the car, my phone rang. Nona's name flashed across the screen. My grandmother basically raised me. I grew up next door and my parents, who owned their own business, farmed out parenting to her. It wasn't a bad way to grow up, but it's resulted in a stilted relationship with them and a great one with her.

"Hi Nona," I said as I opened the call. "How're you?"

"Well, you're working too hard if you just now have time for me on a holiday," she responded. "No one cares how an old bag like me is doing. How's your morning so far, Miss America?"

My Nona was, as one of her friends put it, a hoot. She said whatever was on her mind and always had. She was nosy to a fault; always in everybody else's business. She's probably where I got my incessant need to know everything.

"I mean, I guess I'm okay. I'm covering a major story."

She snorted on the other end of the call.

"What? Somebody's goat had triplets?"

I smiled and had to stifle a laugh. Nona understood my frustrations. I wanted to cover real stories and not the small-town ridiculousness that I usually did. She's the one that encouraged me to follow journalism. When everyone else told me I was stupid to go into a dying industry, she supported me. She's never doubted my abilities for a moment, even when I feel like I'm wholly inadequate. In her world, I'm a Pulitzer Prize winner, even if most of the time I just cover select board meetings.

"Actually, this time it's real. There was a shooting this morning; one person is dead and another was rushed to the hospital. There's a suspect in custody."

"Well slap my ass and call me darlin'," she said. "Somethin' actually happened in that po-dunk town of yours."

My Nona is nothing if not colorful.

"I know. And I've got a feeling that the person the cops have didn't do it. I can't prove it yet, but something in my gut is telling me they're wrong."

I could almost see her nodding on the other end of the line. Nona was short, barely five feet tall, but added some inches because her hair was so big. She subscribed to the idea that *the higher the hair, the closer to God.* And while she swore like a sailor, she prayed the rosary every day and had the 4 PM Monday slot for Eucharistic adoration. She was a character that people almost never believed was real, until they met her. She's larger than life and I miss her every day.

"Well, follow that gut of yours. If it's tellin' you somethin', you listen. If anyone can figure it out, it's my girl."

I could almost see her sitting in her chair in the kitchen, most likely peeling something or rolling pasta dough, pointing a perfectly manicured red finger, caked with flour or starch, in my direction. She would raise one arched eyebrow and wink at me.

"Now I gotta go, my sauce is starting to stick."

She hung up. My family doesn't do a normal Thanksgiving. We just eat Italian food like we do every Sunday. My mom has four brothers and family legend tells that my Uncle Tony asked one year why they didn't eat turkey and dressing. Nona allegedly replied, "we didn't come to this country to eat wet bread." She did cede some ground and started to make the lasagna in a turkey-shaped pan. I'm sure she was cooking away, just waiting for everyone to arrive and gather around her massive dining room table.

This wasn't the first time I was away from home for the holidays. Sure, I missed Nona and my sisters, but I never had the money to come home, or I was working. Plus, I pretty much hated the holidays. I was the black sheep of the family. My older sisters were both in medical school and I had opted off the path and denied my parents the joy of attending law school. We grew up blue collar and all they wanted for us was to *succeed*. Except in my case, they saw journalism as a failure and a waste of my talent. Whatever, I was finally covering something that might get me to a real paper.

I texted my mom, *'Happy Thanksgiving'* and she responded with a picture of the whole family in the kitchen. They all looked happy. If I was home, I would be miserable, wanting to be anywhere but there. In many ways, this was my perfect holiday plan. I mean, without the death and gun violence. I wanted to cover stories like this. I wanted to chase down leads and figure out what the hell was going on, piecing together a story. My phone vibrated and I looked down. It was a text from Michael. The press conference had been set.

I rolled my shoulders and cracked my neck. I put the key in the ignition and drove down the long drive, in the direction of the police station. It was time to get some answers.

Chapter TEN

I pulled up right next to Michael, who was leaning against his Subaru, eating an apple. When I got out of the car, he threw one to me.

"I doubt you've eaten much today and this is a marathon. Fuel up."

I gave him a salute and took a bite. The apple was crisp and crunchy, just a little bit sweet. It wasn't perfectly round, which made me think it came out of the orchard behind Michael's house. One of the perks of living in Vermont is that friends and colleagues come with free produce.

"When does this thing start?" I asked, swallowing a large bite of apple.

Michael chewed and scratched his head.

"Sarah said to get down to the station, that they'd be starting soon. When I tried to go in, they told me to wait."

I leaned against my own car and yawned. The day was barely halfway through, and I was exhausted. I hadn't eaten enough and I needed a trough of coffee.

I thought about what I'd just learned from Colin. He was able to confirm my suspicions. And I got to him before the cops did. I was surprised they didn't immediately look at Nathaniel and Bryon's friends. But what do I know, all my police work knowledge comes from watching too much *Law & Order*.

"Are we going to be the only media present?"

Michael checked his watch, unfolded his arms and legs, before folding them again. He was getting annoyed just standing here.

"I'm hoping. The Rutland Herald doesn't have the manpower to send somebody down here on a holiday and the TV station is all the way in Burlington. I don't think they could get anyone here on time."

I nodded. If we were the only media, that meant that we wouldn't get scooped. I would be pissed if someone stole this story out from under my nose. We already broke what happened, but I had to be the first to publish. TV would get to it before we would be able to print the physical paper, but we could post online. I wasn't going to let someone beat me in my own backyard.

We stood in silence, the easy kind that exists between people that really know each other. I've worked for Michael for 3 years. I've had dinner at his house, and he's bought me a birthday cake. Somedays, it feels like it's just the two of us against the world. We had an easy camaraderie, something I doubted I'd find in any other newsroom. Plus, Michael trusted me. He really wanted me to report and him to edit. He didn't breathe down my neck when I was writing stories. He set firm deadlines and expected me to meet them, but he let me chase stories in my own way.

I was swiping through my email when the door to the police station opened and Sarah walked out. She'd changed out of her long puffer coat and put on a Vermont State

Police jacket. Her hair was no longer loose, instead it was pulled back into a low bun. She meant business.

"We're ready for you both. You're the only press that got here in time."

She was curt, professional. Nothing like she was only a few hours ago. But I expected nothing less. This was her arena, and I was the gladiator entering, trying to win my freedom. I wanted information and she had to protect it. We'd be at odds for the entirety of this press conference and that was all right with me. I was looking forward to sparring with her. She didn't know what I had in my back pocket.

When Michael and I entered the lobby of the police station, it had been spruced up some. There was a card table with a few chairs, as well as a podium. It looked like the podium they used every year on Town Meeting day. Sarah had also put out two chairs for Michael and me in front of the table. It looked a little ridiculous, so formal for two people, but I got what she was going for. She wanted this press conference to be taken seriously. *She* wanted to be taken seriously. I don't blame her; I feel the same way. It's not easy being the only woman in the room; I understood the pressure that puts on you.

We took a seat and Michael started to fiddle with the settings on his camera. We were in our duo-mode, him with a camera to his eye, me with a pen to paper. This is how we worked best, as a team ready to take on the news. Sarah was tapping away on her phone and looked stressed. This would be one of the biggest moments of her career too. She started right after the big drug bust, so she wasn't in charge of the initial press, but had to handle all the rest. She's good at her job. On more than one occasion she's driven me crazy when I was trying to report a story. Today was different though. Today was more than just getting information about a DUI. This was major news, and I was the one to break it.

I wanted to do more than break this story. I wanted to report the shit out of it. I had a feeling the cops were going in the wrong direction, but I also had no idea where to go next. I had to figure out where Nathanial was getting his drugs. If I could find his dealer, I could blow this whole thing open. I knew in my gut that Will wasn't it. He had too much to lose. It was someone else and I was going to be the person to figure it out.

The doors to the rest of the station opened and Chief Strauss, Dickie, and Lieutenant Lyman Collins walked out the door. Each took a seat at the table. The chief nodded to Michael and me and looked nervous. This wasn't his usual rodeo. He was a small-town police chief, usually handling car lockouts and small domestic spats. He knew everyone in town and was able to handle most incidents without an arrest. He and Dickie were a positive—for the most part—presence in town. And I'm sure they both wanted nothing more than to be at home, deep-frying a turkey for both of their families, as was their tradition. I also wanted to be home; except I planned to be in bed today until the lighted tractor parade tomorrow. Instead, I was here wearing yesterday's eyeliner and no bra.

Sarah pocketed her phone and walked over to the men. They all turned away from us as she whispered something to the group. Michael and I shared a look—something happened. And we were about to find out. Sarah stood back up and walked towards the podium. She cleared her throat and gripped the sides of the podium. She was nervous. I turned on the recording app on my phone. *Go time.*

"I want to thank you both for being here today. We'll hear from Chief Strauss and Lieutenant Collins before opening up for questions. While we have a small group today, I would still appreciate it if you both held your questions until I open up the floor."

Sarah looked at Michael and I, as if awaiting a response. We both nodded and she continued on.

"I will welcome Chief Bernard Strauss first. Chief."

She stepped away from the podium and the chief stood up from the folding chair where he sat. He looked nervous, even though it was only Michael and I in the room. I can't tell you how many conversations we've had between the three of us. But this time, there is a separation; he was on one side of the table as part of the investigation and we were on the other side as the press. No more hometown loyalty. Sarah was sure to make it seem like we were playing on opposing teams. What she didn't realize was I came to play ball.

The chief made his way to the podium and leaned against it. There was the creak of wood while he stood awkwardly, shifting his weight from foot to foot. He looked over at Sarah.

"Is this necessary? It's just Michael and Alice."

She gave him a look that said, *'don't fucking push me,'* and he just shook his head. The man was obviously uncomfortable. I don't blame him. I didn't feel so comfy myself, but I wasn't going to let them know that. This was my first real press conference as a real journalist. Sure, I'd been to a few as a student, but nothing like this. Me and Bernie were in the same boat. I was nervous too. I was afraid I wouldn't ask the right questions or not get the answers I needed. He cleared his throat.

"I guess I'll begin. I'm Bernie Strauss, but you two already know that," he said nervously. The chief looked over at Sarah and she nodded encouragingly. He cleared his throat again and tugged at his collar.

"Around 6 AM this morning, I stopped into the police station to just check in on everything. My dispatch alerted me to the 911 call made about shooting at Bedford Farm. Officer Jack Campbell initially reported to the scene, where he discovered two victims. He immediately called for backup and EMS. Myself and Dickie responded."

The chief's forehead was slick with sweat and he reached into his pocket to pull out a handkerchief. He mopped his brow and wiped his mouth. After adjusting his glasses, he continued.

"When we arrived at Bedford Farm, we immediately began first aid on both victims. Unfortunately, one was already dead when we arrived. Dickie called for more backup and dispatch alerted the state police. We were able to stabilize the second victim as much as possible before EMS brought him to the Black River Health Clinic. He was then picked up by DART, the air ambulance, and transported to Dartmouth Hitchcock Medical Center."

Bernie looked over at Sarah, who nodded her approval. For a man as nervous as him, he did a great job. Michael kept clicking away, taking photos, while Lieutenant Collins stood. Bernie moved to sit down, and the Lieutenant went to the podium.

"This is where I pick up," Lieutenant Collins said. "We received a call at approximately 6:30 AM this morning for additional backup and our rapid response crime team to deploy to 100 Route 11 in Black River, the aforementioned Bedford Farm. We arrived at the scene where local officers were already at work. We will officially take over the investigation at this point, as is protocol, but Chief Strauss and his department are still an extremely important part of the investigation."

He too looked over at Sarah and she nodded. He sat back down, and she came to the podium. So far, I've learned nothing, but I hoped she would open for questions. I had been on scene, so I witnessed everything firsthand, but I needed the victims' names released officially. I mean, the whole town probably already knew what happened, but I wanted to break the story and report who was dead or alive. Sarah cleared her throat.

"We will now release the names of the victims. Unfortunately, this is now a double homicide; we just found out the second victim did not make it through emergency surgery."

The police station got quiet. Michael stopped taking pictures, the shutter of his camera falling silent. This just got more serious. A double homicide? I mean, it was always bad, but now there were two people dead. Two teenagers dead. Who did it?

"Byron Avery, seventeen, perished at the scene, while Nathaniel Bedford, also seventeen, perished during surgery. Both are from town and were students at Andover. I have a statement from the families that I will read now."

She pulled her phone out of her pocket and swiped it open. I'm sure the statement came from the Senator. This had his handwriting all over it. Who else would think to release a statement when their child died? Sarah took a beat before she began reading.

"Today, through a senseless act of violence, two upstanding young men were taken from this community. Nathanial Bedford and Byron Avery were both bright individuals with nothing but potential. Their young lives were cut short, and we lost them far too soon. As separate families, we hope to grieve in private, but understand that the loss of our boys is also a loss for the whole community. It is our hope that their killer be brought to justice. The Bedford and Avery families."

Everyone was silent after that, not sure of how to proceed. As the silence stretched, it became awkward, and I had to cut the tension. So, I did what anyone would do and raised my hand like I was a fourth-grader.

"Alice," Sarah said, lifting one eyebrow.

"Is it time for questions?"

Sarah's face was hard to read, but she quickly pasted on a professional smile across her face. It was as if she thought she could get through this press conference without hearing from me, which was a ridiculous thought. I had what felt like hundreds of questions on the tip of my tongue and I wanted to ask them now.

"Of course, Alice. We can open the floor to questions."

The chief shook his head, as if he was annoyed. I didn't blame him. This formality seemed silly—Michael and I were the only press present. We all knew each other, and knew each other well. I mean, I've seen Sarah naked for Christ's sake.

"Do we have to have this song and dance? Can't we just talk?" he asked.

Now it was Sarah's turn to look annoyed. She wanted this press conference to run as if it was a real one. Which it was, but we were the only press. We were all friendly. There was no point in the whole dog and pony show. But I respected what she wanted to do. She wanted to be seen as a professional, and to do that she needed to run the show. But at the same time, she also realized this was a pretty unique situation, where formalities seemed to be a bit much. She sighed and shook her head. I could tell she was forcing herself not to roll her eyes.

"Go ahead. Just talk to each other."

Sarah went and sat on the last chair at the table. Michael dropped the camera from his eye and sat quietly next to me. This was officially my show.

"I have quite a few questions, but first, why was Will Ward arrested? He has an alibi for the time of the crime."

Sarah was already annoyed, but now she was stewing. I didn't mince words. I wasn't here to mess around. I wanted answers and I wanted them *now*. Both the chief and lieutenant looked at each other and then at Sarah. She just shrugged, as if to say, '*you wanted it casual.*'

The chief cleared his throat. "Where'd you hear that, Alice?"

I smirked. He knew better than anyone that I didn't have to reveal my sources. This would not be the first time I've come to the chief with information from a source that he's had to answer. He sighed and took off his glasses, before he gestured to the lieutenant to answer.

"Well, Alice, we had it on good authority that Mr. Ward was a person of interest and after bringing him in, we had enough to arrest him for the crime. He will be officially charged after the holiday."

I narrowed my eyes and looked over to Sarah. She was looking everywhere but at me. She knew it was wrong to arrest Will, just like I did. I needed more information.

"But what information would that be? Will has a solid alibi for last night and this morning."

Lieutenant Collins squirmed in his seat. He knew I had him. He knew he didn't have an answer to this question. And he knew that I knew he didn't have an answer.

"Well Alice, this is an ongoing investigation, and I don't have to answer that."

Ongoing investigation my ass.

Chapter ELEVEN

I kept peppering them with questions. Why did they think this was a drug related crime? What evidence pointed to that? How did they know it wasn't just the annual party getting out of control? What about Marla Ward's alibi for her brother?

"I have it on good authority from a source that Nathaniel had a local drug connection. I know you think that this person is Will Ward, but he was never more than an addict and I also know he stopped buying the boys' pot. Why would he be selling something harder? Why are you discounting another source?"

The lieutenant went to open his mouth, but I cut him off.

"Along with that, the main dealer in town was never caught and drugs still flow into Black River, specifically pills. Will Ward wasn't a pill head, he was a known heroin user. Again, where do you think the drugs are coming from and why do you think it's Will?"

Sarah glanced my way. We shared a look that made me think I was on the right track. She barely nodded her head, but it was there, just for me. I knew I was close. Someone was going to give me the information I needed.

"I'll handle this one," the chief said to the lieutenant. "Alice, you've risen some good points, but this is an investigation. And we're *investigating*. There is evidence that points to Will. And we are exploring that evidence. We don't have to tell you anything else."

I was officially annoyed. I knew they weren't going to tell me, but this was bullshit. I knew they had the wrong guy; I just couldn't prove it yet.

"I understand this is an active investigation and you don't have to tell me shit. But I also have *evidence*. I also have *information*. And what you're telling me doesn't add up."

There was silence in the room. Michael was still beside me, his hands resting in his lap. I wondered if he thought I was taking it too far, but as of right now, he wasn't stepping in to stop me. So, I pushed even more.

"Has anyone been able to account for the whereabouts of Bobby Bedford? Have you looked at any of the guns in his house to compare to what was found at the scene of the crime?"

Shock, anger, and annoyance passed over everyone's faces. But Dickie also gave away surprise and looked at me with his mouth open.

"Alice, that's an accusation that you don't want to be making," he said, shifting in his seat.

All three men were uncomfortable. The Bedford's were powerful in town. The name meant something; it had weight behind it. And I opened my mouth, asking a question I knew they weren't going to answer, but still needed to be asked. I kept pushing.

"If you're looking at all angles, shouldn't you look

towards the family? Aren't most violent crimes committed by someone close to the victim? Bobby Bedford has a known issue with alcohol and a bad temper. Why isn't he being considered?"

Michael cleared his throat, but he didn't interrupt. I knew I was skating on thin ice. I knew I had to be careful when I spoke next, but I also tend to have a *bull in the china shop* mentality sometimes. Fuck, the Bedford's already hated me. The Senator wanted to shut me up. I might as well ask the damn questions.

"Bobby Bedford didn't go to the hospital with his wife. He had easy access to the barns. He knows where the security cameras are and where they point. He owns firearms. And he was drunk this morning, meaning he was probably drunk last night. When I spoke to him earlier today, he didn't have anything nice to say about his son. Why aren't you considering him?"

Bernie's face was as bright as a tomato. He shifted in his seat and looked at the Lieutenant, throwing up his hands.

"This is your rodeo now. And this is off the record, Alice. But she's got a point," he said.

Sarah audibly groaned. Her tenuous grasp on the situation was slipping through her fingers. I had to press. I had to know more. I was digging myself a hole and looking possibly in the right direction, so I kept going.

"We know the dealer is local because Nathaniel had easy access to drugs and didn't have to travel far to pick them up. If you're not going to consider Bobby Bedford as a suspect, why haven't you started to question other low-level dealers in the area. I can think of three or four who could probably provide you with some interesting information."

This was a complete bluff. Sure, I knew who the dealers were in town, everyone did. I also knew they wouldn't talk to the cops. Maybe they would talk to me, but I doubted it. I wanted them to think I had more than I did.

The lieutenant sighed and rubbed at his temples. I finally shut my mouth and Michael continued to sit quietly, listening and observing. I opened my mouth to speak, and the lieutenant raised his hand.

"Alice, what we have is an active investigation. We don't even have autopsy results yet. We don't have any information about the gun used. We're still at the beginning of the process. And I don't have answers for you and even if I did, I don't have to tell you. You are here as a courtesy. Remember that."

Now I was the annoyed one. No one gets to tell me to sit down and shut the fuck up on my turf. I wasn't going down without a fight. He just didn't realize it yet. The chief knew and he leaned back in his chair, his eyes on me, ready for me to go. I smiled sweetly at the lieutenant.

"Lieutenant, I appreciate that you are in the beginning of the investigative process. I understand you don't owe me anything. But you need to understand something. You've got the wrong guy in custody. A killer is out there, biding their time. And I'm pretty sure I'm going to figure it out before you. So, sit back in your chair and be annoyed with me all you want. I'm a damn good reporter. And pardon my French, but you can fuck right off."

I smiled again and stood up, turning to leave. I slammed the door on my way out. Childish, yes. But it sure felt good.

I walked over to my car and unlocked it, but didn't get right in. I leaned against it, my head in my hands. I was tired. I was hungry. I was wearing yesterday's pants and hadn't brushed my teeth. I'd seen a dead body and was certain that the guy in custody was innocent. I just had to find out who actually committed the crime. If I was going to report this story, I was also going to have to investigate it.

That's when I had an idea. I tapped my reporter's notebook against the roof of my car before I slid into the driver's seat. Without waiting for Michael to leave the station, I sped off. I had a hunch that I needed to chase down.

Chapter
TWELVE

I drove out past Bedford Farms and continued for almost fifteen minutes before I took a right down a dirt road. The drive led to a small house—more of a cottage really—with a front porch that had a golden retriever sitting on it. There was smoke coming from the chimney. It was picturesque in that quaint Vermont way. A romantic view of a place that was actually incredibly hard to live.

Before I could even get out of the car, Otis Blackwood stepped out onto the porch. The golden retriever sat up and Otis patted them on the head.

"Hey there, Alice! What brings you out this way?"

Otis was an older man in suspenders, a red flannel shirt, and a pair of dungarees. There were glasses around his neck, the kind that were held together by magnets at the nose, so the wearer could rest them on their neck when not in use. He was old-school Vermont, so ingrained in Black River that he didn't know where his people came before that.

"I've got some questions. Do you mind answering?"

He waved me to come in and I followed him into the

house, stopping for a moment to pet Ellie, his dog. The inside of the house was cozy, worn but perfectly neat. There was a thick, obviously hand sewn quilt on the back of the couch and a fire crackling in the fireplace. His wife, a short woman in an apron, was peeling potatoes.

"Hi Mrs. Blackwood," I said as I walked into the kitchen. Otis motioned for me to sit down, his wife dropped her potatoes and wiped her hands on the apron.

"Alice, how lovely. What can we do for you?"

She smiled in a way that reached her eyes, crinkling at the corners. She was a woman that spent a lot of time smiling, evident from the lines on her face. Otis was similarly weathered, but his came from working outside for decades. His cheeks were constantly red, as if they got chapped thirty years ago and never really got better. He's still working at Bedford Farms as the farm manager. I doubted he would ever retire; he'd die with a rake in his hand, cleaning out a stall.

"Did you hear what happened at Bedford's this morning?" I asked.

Mrs. Blackwood nodded solemnly, the smile falling from her face.

"We did. Such a shame, those boys had problems, but they were just boys."

She took a pot of coffee from the stove and placed a cup in front of me. There were also scones on the table, which she handed me with a small plate. They smelled divine and were still warm. After taking a bite, I smiled.

"Mrs. B, these are amazing."

She smiled and sat down next to Otis.

"What do you want to know, Alice? I doubt the cops are doin' much."

Otis was one of those guys who had a healthy distrust of

authority. He respected you if you respected him. And I knew for a fact he didn't really respect Chief and Dickie. Especially after everything Will went through. Otis hired Will off and on for years, mostly to help do random projects when he needed an extra set of hands. But ever since Will got clean, he's been an actual employee at Bedford's. Apparently, he's good at tractor maintenance.

"Do you mind if I record this? Just so I make sure I get all the information?"

He nodded. Mrs. Blackwood took a sip of coffee and daintily wiped her mouth with a cloth napkin. Otis nodded and I pulled my phone out of my pocket. I started the recording and set my phone on the table. The pen jammed in my bun was retrieved and I got my notebook out of the back pocket of my jeans.

"How did you find out about what happened?"

Otis scratched his head and told me that Marla called not long after Will was picked up by the cops. He heard about the shooting like everyone else had, from the police scanner.

"I'm still tryin' to understand their rationale. Will has made mistakes in the past, that's undeniable. But the boy is clean, he's got a job, he's a functional, tax-paying member of society. They're looking for an easy scapegoat," he said.

I nodded, jotting down some notes.

"Otis, you know everyone. Do you have any idea how Nathaniel and Byron may have sourced drugs? Even just a hunch or a rumor could be helpful at this point."

He looked out into the middle distance for a moment before answering. I could tell the man was going through interactions and memories, trying to come up with something that could potentially help.

"I can tell you—without a doubt—it's not Will. And I

don't think it's from the usual suspects in town. Someone else has something going on. I wish I had more to tell you."

I sat quietly, thinking. It was a long-shot question. Otis was one of those guys that knew everyone and noticed everything. If anyone had a hunch about where the drugs were coming from, it would be him. I took another bite of my scone and we all sat in companionable silence.

"Have you spoken with the neighbors?" Mrs. Blackwood asked.

I shook my head no. I hadn't made the rounds to the properties closest to the Bedford's yet. I debated earlier with going over there, because it wasn't likely anyone noticed anything, but maybe that was what I needed.

"Before I go, do you know if Will had access to firearms?" I asked.

"Absolutely not. Marla wouldn't have it. And Will never had the stomach for hunting."

That's what I thought. So, he would've had to go out, purchase a firearm, just to kill two teenage boys? The cop's case was already thin, but it was losing weight quickly, the more questions I asked. I slipped the pen pack into my hair and closed my notebook. But I didn't stop the recording yet.

"Otis, I know there's cameras in the birthing stalls in the barn, but are there cameras anywhere else in the barns?" I asked.

He nodded emphatically.

"Sure are. We just put them in last week. I'm the only one that knows where they are."

I stilled. There were cameras. *In the barn.* Where two boys were shot.

"And do the cops know this?"

Otis smiled. "You're the first one to ask."

Chapter THIRTEEN

I followed Otis back to Bedford Farms and drove around the back. There weren't any cops that we could see, but there was still plastic sheeting and police tape over the front of the barn. There's a small cottage towards the back of the retail space, in between that and the main barn, that Otis works out of. It's basically a tool shed, but it looks fancy on the outside to add to the rural charm of the farm.

We got out of our respective cars and walked to the door, which Otis unlocked. It was cold inside, but just as neat as his house. Every tool was in order and the old metal desk in the corner had a computer, a cup holding pencils, and a yellow legal pad with what looked like a to-do list. Otis sat down in the desk chair, and I looked over at the list. I smiled. Much like me, Otis had his own shorthand that only he could decipher. The list was gibberish to everyone but him.

He fired up the computer and we waited while the program loaded.

"How many cameras are there?"

"We just installed nine. They're all over the barn," he said.

I was vibrating with pure energy. This was evidence that could prove Will innocent. That could find the actual killer. And I had it.

"I'll be right back."

I went out to my car and pulled my backpack from the passenger's seat. I ripped it open and dug around the detritus of my life. There were pens, gum wrappers, and hair ties, as well as an assortment of notebooks. Eventually, in one of the inside pockets, I found what I was looking for. A USB drive.

By the time I got back into Otis' office, the cameras were up and running. They all had different views of the barn, including at the front entrance.

"Why haven't you told the cops? No judgement, I'm just curious," I asked.

He sighed and ran a hand down his face.

"You know Alice, I was waiting for Will to get a lawyer. Marla called me when he got picked up and that's when I thought of the cameras. But I wanted someone to see if it could help Will before I turned them over. I don't know what's on here."

No disrespect to the police force, but how did they not notice there were security cameras? How could they have missed that important detail?

"How are the cameras situated? How come the cops missed them?"

"Well, they're all small to begin with, because we didn't want them noticeable when folks tour the barn. And they're up in the rafters, so unless you know where to look, they're basically invisible," he said.

I thought about this. Security cameras that were just

put in. Whoever shot the boys didn't know they were being recorded. The old-timers at The Kwik only knew about the cameras at the back door of the store and in the birthing stalls. This could be the thing that blows this case wide open.

Otis clicked a few buttons, and a new set of windows opened up. Nine boxes for the nine different cameras, all with different angles of the barn. Otis tapped a few more keys and fast-forwarded until 5:30 AM this morning. I was impressed with his technical skills. I guess you can teach an old dog new tricks.

We watched together as the minutes passed, with absolutely nothing happening in the barn. There were cows, but that was it. But then at 5:51 AM, two boys entered the barn through the front door. It was Nathaniel and Byron. There was no sound, but they looked agitated, like they were in the middle of some kind of disagreement. They fought silently for a minute before their attention was drawn elsewhere, outside the barn.

This was it. The tension in the room was palpable. We were about to watch the boys get shot and hopefully get a look at the shooter. Byron stepped back and Nathaniel took the lead, arguing with whoever was on the outside of the barn. And then they walked in the frame. Whoever it was small, short in stature and dressed like everyone else in town: thick winter coat and a beanie. They were facing the other direction from this camera angle, so we couldn't see their face.

I looked at all the boxes, hoping to get a full look at the mystery person. They were facing another camera, but were in a shadow in the barn, so I couldn't make them out. We were both completely still, waiting to see what would happen. Then there was a flash and Byron fell. Nathaniel turned to look at his friend and raised his hands to whoever was in the shadows. His body language went from irritated to scared. It was like he lost years of his life and wasn't a cocky teenager anymore, but a terrified little boy. With his hands up, he was attempting to speak to whoever held the gun. Whatever he said didn't work. There was another flash and Nathaniel crumpled.

We had the crime on tape. I watched intently, hoping whoever it was would leave the shadows and turn, just enough to catch a glimpse. There was a beat, and then another, and whoever it was walked out. They had a bit of a limp, as if they weren't bending their knee to walk and instead picking up their leg from the hip. It was slight, barely noticeable. But it pinged something in the back of my head. I just didn't know *what.*

Otis turned to face me.

"Well, the cameras caught it."

I handed him the USB drive.

"Can you put the footage on here? And can you give me an hour before you send it to the cops?"

He took the small drive, put it in the computer and moved some files around. We watched the file transfer from the program to my drive. When it chimed that it was complete, he turned to me and handed me the evidence.

"You've got an hour, kid. Make it count."

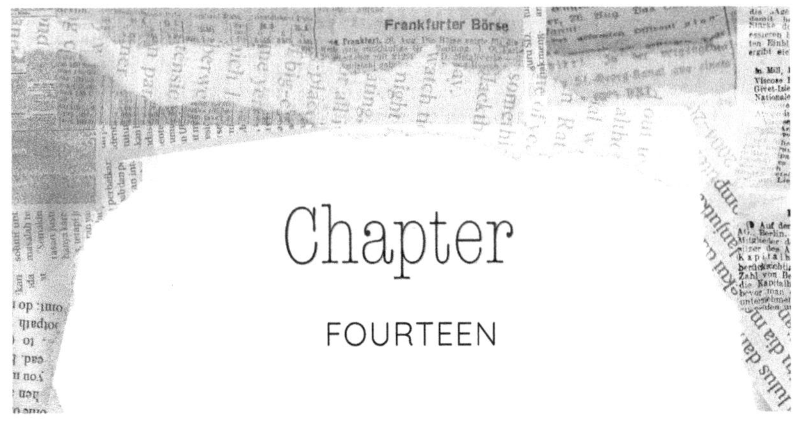

Chapter FOURTEEN

I drove out of Bedford Farms and immediately went back to the office. It only took about ten minutes, but that was valuable time. I found Michael at his desk, going through photos for the front page. I pulled the flash drive out of my pocket and threw it at him. He caught it with his left hand, without taking his eyes away from the computer screen. He scrunched his face up in confusion when he saw what he caught.

"And why are we throwing flash drives, Alice?"

I realized I was shaking all over. Adrenaline was pumping in my veins. I couldn't catch my breath. I felt like I might be having a panic attack, except I also felt oddly calm. I had something here. I wasn't quite sure what it was yet, but I had *something*. I started pacing between our desks.

"What you are holding in your hands is surveillance footage of the murders."

I let that soak in for a moment. Michael looked from me to his hand and back at me. His eyes narrowed.

"How did you get this?"

I knew he would ask. And I could trust Michael. Plus,

Otis would be turning this over to the police, so I didn't necessarily need to protect him as an anonymous source.

"Otis just installed security cameras. No one knows about them but him and I'm assuming Bobby Bedford. Start watching at 5:51 AM. You'll see the whole thing."

Michael inserted the drive into his computer and opened up the file. I stood behind him while he watched. I rocked back and forth on my heels, unable to stop moving. After the gunshots, I paid close attention to the shooter walking away. I knew I recognized that walk, but I just wasn't sure where.

"Do the police have this?" Michael asked me, turning around to look at me.

I shook my head no.

"I told Otis to wait an hour before he hands it over."

Michael frowned. I could tell he wasn't too keen on keeping something from the police—but at the same time—this was a major break in the story. This was proof that it wasn't Will. The shooter on the screen was too short in stature. Will is tall and lanky and definitely doesn't match whoever pulled the trigger.

"I know. I know... He's turning it over. But I just need a little more time to chase down leads. I'm so close to getting this story."

Michael took off his reading glasses and looked at me, folding his arms over his chest. I could tell he was weighing what I said. On one hand, this was evidence in an active murder investigation. On the other hand, this was the biggest story to ever come out of Black River and breaking this news would be huge get for the paper. I wasn't sure the ethics behind this or even the legality, but I knew I wanted to run this down before the cops got involved. Because once they did, my story was done.

I look back over to the screen, where Michael had paused the video. That short person with a slight limp looked familiar but I couldn't place why. I looked up at the ceiling and rubbed my eyes. Then I had it.

I raced over to my desk and grabbed my keys and notebook. I started out the door, without saying a word to Michael.

"Alice, where are you going?" He yelled at me as I went to open the door.

My hand on the handle, I turned to look at him.

"I gotta go. I think I know what happened."

And with that, I ran out of the newsroom and to my car.

I TOOK a deep breath and pushed myself back into my seat, my hands clutching the steering wheel. I was about to report the biggest story of my life. Or I was about to end up dead. I really didn't know which. Because I was pretty sure I knew who pulled the trigger. And I was sitting in her driveway.

I got out of my car and gently closed the door, letting my hands rest against its cold shell. This was it. This was my make-or-break moment. I was officially moving from staff writer to investigative reporter. That is, if I wasn't wrong. I could be completely off-base and about to accuse someone innocent of a heinous crime. But it was a shot I was willing to take.

Before I walked to the front door, I studied the small, white house. It was like so many other colonials in the area. Painted white with an old red barn behind it, there were two large maple trees in the front yard, both with just the smallest bit of snow clinging to their bare branches. What I was about to do, what I was walking into could potentially be both stupid and dangerous. I figured someone needed to know where I was. I swiped open my phone and hovered between two names, unsure of who to tell. One was safer. One was a risk. I went with the latter.

I'm at Irma Grey's. If you don't hear from me in about 20 minutes, get over here. It's important. I'll explain later.

Irma Grey is one of those stereotypical, weathered Vermonters. She's steadfast, has an elaborate garden, and sends in recipes to be printed in The Black River Recorder. Except she doesn't have a computer or know how to use one, so she handwrites her recipes, and I type them up for her. She comes into the office a few times a month. And she walks with a slight limp, as if she's not totally bending her knee and lifting her leg from her hip.

I walked through the yard, the leftover frozen snow crunching beneath my boots. When I got to the door, I took a deep breath to steel myself. My hands were shaking, my heart was beating so hard I thought it might jump out of my chest. I raised my hand to knock, and the door swung open.

A short, older lady stood in front of me. She had white-blonde hair cropped close to her scalp. Her face was weathered from time and the elements, and her hands were gnarled. She wore a turkey sweatshirt to celebrate the day, which I kept forgetting was Thanksgiving. And she looked like she was expecting me. She smiled, but it didn't reach her eyes.

"Took you long enough. Come on in out of the cold," she said and stepped away from the door, waving for me to follow.

I took a hesitant step into the house. It was simple but clean. There weren't family pictures on every surface, a warm fire in the hearth, or a half-chewed dog toy. This place was sterile, with no personality or warmth. It wasn't a home; this was just a house someone lived in. Irma walked back through a small hallway, and I followed, ending up in a large, airy kitchen. Again, it was well arranged, but it felt like no one had ever made anything more than a microwaved Lean Cuisine in it.

She gestured towards a seat at the large, circular kitchen table and I moved to sit down. We sat in silence for what felt like eons. I tried to say something multiple times but shut my mouth each time. Finally, I pulled my phone from my pocket and ignored multiple texts from Sarah. I opened my recording app and placed my phone on the table between us.

"Do you mind if I record this? Whatever you say can be used in my story, and I'll run a recording so I can make sure I get your direct quotes correct. Is that okay?"

Irma looked at me in a way that no one ever had before. It was like she was trying to see through my skull and into my brain, as if to see what I was thinking. She stared at me for what felt like hours but was probably just a few moments. Then she looked down at her hands, shrugged, and looked back at me.

"Fire it up. It's time this story gets told."

Chapter FIFTEEN

Irma opened her mouth to speak, paused, thought for a moment with her head tilted, and then sighed. She looked back at me and everything came out.

"My husband died ten years ago. I didn't know how bad off we were. I never looked at the finances, that was his job. So, when he died, there were taxes and loans, all sorts of bills piled up. Not too long after, I fell and busted my knee. I was laid up for weeks, dodging calls from the bank. They didn't take the house, but they threatened to. So, I sold some land to take off some of the pressure, but it just wasn't enough.

"When I broke my knee, they kept prescribing pain medication. Nasty stuff. I couldn't take it. But Medicare covered it, and the pharmacy delivered it every month, so I just socked it away in a drawer. Then one night, I watched 60 Minutes, and they were talkin' about how much money there was in the heroin trade. People want that, they want Fentanyl, they want pills. They want a fix, they want it now, and they'll pay for it.

"So, I got to thinkin' and I realized just how much I had. I was sitting on money that could solve all my problems. I was gonna *lose* the house. So, I did what I had to do. I'm not proud of it, but I had no option.

"My grandson, Dennis, he had friends that would buy from me. It started small. I made just enough to keep the bank off my back. So, I'd go to the doctor, complain about the pain, and get more pills. He never suspected a thing. What little old lady would lie?

"But I needed more; I got some other folks involved. I had them complain of pain, and they would get pills. The pills are covered, but I'd send them a little cash for their trouble. They told their friends, who told their friends. I have a whole network getting pills for me. We were getting just enough that I paid off all the bills and was able to eat food other than tuna and noodles again. I wasn't gettin' rich, but I wasn't drownin' either.

"Then Nathaniel came back from school. He'd been to rehab the summer before and stayed on the straight and narrow during the school year. But somehow, he caught wind that I had pills that could make the pain go away. Usually, Dennis handled the selling. But Nathaniel came straight to me. He just knocked on my door and made a demand. He also threatened to turn me in.

"So, I did what anyone would do in that situation—I sold to him. Every few days at first and then every day, he would show up, lookin'. I stopped selling to everyone but him. He just kept throwing money my way. I was able to buy back the part of the land that I sold off to pay the property taxes.

"He started to get demanding. I couldn't keep up. I told him, but he wouldn't accept that. In his mind, pills weren't that big of a deal, so he wasn't *really* a drug addict. But he was far gone. That was all this past summer. I breathed a sigh of relief when he left for school in the fall. I was still able to sell, but he wasn't knocking on my door at all hours of the night, lookin' to score.

"Until the other day. He got back for break and headed straight to me. And he started demanding immediately. What he doesn't know is I was lookin' to stop. I paid off what needed to be paid off. I'm an eighty-five year-old woman. I'm tired. I didn't want to worry about supply and getting caught. I tried to tell him, but he didn't want to hear it. He was frantic and he kept sneaking away to come over here. I sold him the last bit of pills I had but it wasn't enough.

"Nathaniel was a problem, and he was going to continue to be. After the last night, when he was knocking at my front door so hard I thought it would fall down, I followed him back to Bedford's. He ducked into the barn and Byron was there as well. What those idiots were doing, drunk in the barn was beyond me. But there they were.

"I'll say this, and I want you to believe me when I say it, I didn't *mean* to kill them. I thought I would just wound them enough to leave me alone. But my eyesight must still be pretty good because I hit both of them square in the chest. *I did it.* I got out of my car, argued with Nathaniel and shot Byron to get him to shut up. Nathaniel kept whining, demanding I sell to him. So, I shot him too. And then I got back in my car and drove up the street to my house. I called 911 from that phone over there."

She pointed to a kitchen phone that looked like it had been hanging in the same spot since the 1950s. Who even still has a landline? Irma leaned back and looked at me. I glanced down at my phone, making sure it had been recording the whole time.

"May I ask a question?"

She nodded, her gaze never leaving mine.

"Why are you telling me all this? Why didn't you just go to the cops?"

Irma laughed and picked at nonexistent lint on her slacks. She sat in silence for a moment before she answered, as if she was weighing her words carefully.

"Alice, we don't really know each other. But you're a straight-shooter. I've seen you at selectboard meetings. You don't take bullshit, and you write what happened. The cops are gonna twist it. They're gonna spin some tale. But you? You're gonna get the facts straight."

This was a weird time to get it, but this was pretty much the best compliment I've ever gotten in my journalistic career. It's just too bad it came from the mouth of a drug dealing, murderous grandmother.

"Now it's my turn to ask a question. How did you figure it out?" she asked, one eyebrow cocked.

"Cameras were recently installed in the barns at Bedford Farms, the whole thing was caught. You can't make out your face, but I figured out it was you from your limp."

She smiled but it didn't reach her eyes.

"Smart girl," she said, pointing a knobby finger in my direction.

I stopped the recording and noticed multiple missed texts from Sarah. I raised my phone and pointed to it.

"I've got to make a call."

She waved me away and I dialed Sarah while I walked out front. She picked up on the first ring.

"What the hell, Alice? Why did you text me like that? Are you okay?"

There was genuine concern, almost panic in her voice. Maybe we would be something.

"I'm fine, really. I'm at Irma Grey's. You're gonna want to get down here with everyone. I got a story—"

Before I could finish my thought, the still November afternoon was shattered by a single gunshot. It sounded like it came from the kitchen.

ABOUT THE AUTHOR

Anna M. Boarini was a girl who loved books and grew up to become a woman who writes them. Much like Elizabeth Bennet, she's very fond of walking. You can follow her work at annaboarini.com. On The Record is her first book.

www.ingramcontent.com/pod-product-compliance
Lightning Source LLC
Chambersburg PA
CBHW060548310726
48982CB00008B/1053/J

* 9 7 9 8 9 9 9 6 6 2 2 0 0 *